I0709334

USA TODAY BESTSELLING AUTHOR

Dale Mayer

TERK'S GUARDIANS
WALKER 05

WALKER: TERK'S GUARDIANS, BOOK 5
Beverly Dale Mayer
Valley Publishing Ltd.

Copyright © 2024 Beverly Dale Mayer

All rights reserved. Except for use in any review, the reproduction or utilization of this work in whole or in part by any electronic, mechanical or other means, now known or hereafter invented, including xerography, photocopying and recording, or in any information storage or retrieval system, is forbidden without the written permission of the publisher.

This is a work of fiction. Names, characters, places, brands, media, and incidents are either the product of the author's imagination or are used fictitiously. Any resemblance to actual events, locales, or persons, living or dead, is entirely coincidental.

ISBN-13: 978-1-778863-06-6
Print Edition

Books in This Series:

Radar, Book 1

Legend, Book 2

Bojan, Book 3

Langdon, Book 4

Walker, Book 5

Reid, Book 6

Sanders, Book 7

Nate, Book 8

About This Book

Having precog abilities didn't guarantee having answers, but it did mean Walker knew when trouble was in a specific area. In this case it was Finland and involved someone associated with Levi and a friend to Walker. So he wants in on this job – even if Levi doesn't have a job there. Yet. However, a quick phone call to Terk confirms Walker's suspicions. And he's already on the move.

Ashley's life should have eased up with her move to Finland, but that same wariness creeping back in her life made her feel hunted once again. A strong healer, she helped those who showed up on her doorstep, telling them that she believed the healing energy brought them to her.

However, she'd long ago learned that not everyone who showed up at her house wanted the best for her. So, when Walker shows up, she's not sure what to believe, but it's quickly all too clear that her life is in danger.

Should she trust Walker? No, but she has to make a choice, and the wrong one could kill her …

Sign up to be notified of all Dale's releases here!
https://geni.us/DaleNews

PROLOGUE

R IFF SAT ACROSS the table and stared at Terk, the others quietly watching. "So, what? Did you get anywhere?"

"It's still in progress," Tasha noted, from his side. "It's not been all that easy to find information."

"That's because we're sitting here," Riff snapped, "doing nothing."

"It's true that we are here, and sitting, but we're certainly not doing *nothing*," Terk clarified. "You also know that things happen in their own time."

Riff glared at him. "Sounds like an excuse to me."

At that, Terk shot him a look and took a breath. "Come on, Riff. It's not an excuse, and you and I both know it."

"Yes, but I'm damn impatient."

"I know, with good cause. We're also getting a lot of phone calls from Angela."

Riff frowned at that and looked off in the distance.

"What's the relationship between you two?"

"Complex," he snapped.

At that, several people around the table laughed.

"Yeah, that's something we've all dealt with," Terk shared, with a smile. "It doesn't necessarily wash though."

"Fine," Riff grumbled. "I'll wait a little bit longer."

"And Angela?" Celia asked, patting her belly. "She seems to think she will be needed."

Riff winced.

"If she is, you would be the best bet to contact her," Terk suggested to Riff, but Riff seemed to want to be anywhere but here. "I understand that she's very, very good at what she does."

"Is she like us?" Cara asked, looking at Riff intently. He gave her a reluctant nod. "She's a healer then?" Cara and Clary looked over at Riff with interest.

"We can always use more healers." Clary liked that prospect.

"You don't want her," Riff declared.

"Why is that?" she asked.

"She'll organize your life away," he replied, with a wave of his hand. "She'll get in your face, and you won't know whether you're coming or going."

At that, Cara nodded slowly. "I see."

"No, you don't see," Riff snapped, glaring. "You don't see anything."

"Yeah, I do," she argued. "I think we should probably meet her." She turned to Terk.

Terk studied Riff. "It's probably a good idea, even if it's not today. Maybe in a few days or even a couple weeks."

"That's possible," Cara noted, with a nod as she assessed the room. "It's probably good timing, but we don't want her too early."

"No, we don't, and, if she knows when to come, it won't matter what you say," Riff declared, looking at her. "She'll be here regardless, and, when you see her, you'll know you're heading for trouble."

"Trouble or just the timing of things?" Cara asked.

Riff shrugged. "I see her, and it means trouble, so who knows. It depends on the relationship you have with her," he muttered.

At that, Cara could hardly hide her smile.

Terk looked around the room, recognizing what the others also recognized, but what Riff was desperately trying not to. Terk realized there would be yet another relationship happening, but it just wasn't time yet.

Terk's phone rang, and he looked down at the screen to see who was calling. "Hey, Levi. How's life?"

"Everything is fine here, but maybe I should ask you how it's going on your end."

Terk assessed it for a moment, then replied, "I would have said all is tickety-boo over here, at least for the moment. How about you?"

"Nope, all good on our side," Levi replied.

"So … why are you calling then?"

"What? Can't a friend just call?"

"Yep, you sure can. But what's up?"

Levi hesitated. "Somebody contacted me about some work, and, in my research, we came up with something that's a bit off," he shared. "I'm wondering if he is one of yours."

"One of mine? That would be interesting. Why? You don't need him?"

"I could use him, yeah, but I was wondering if anybody wanted to join in and see, … you know, maybe test this guy out and confirm whether he's one of yours or I can hire him over at my end. I always feel guilty keeping the psychic ones."

"You haven't managed to keep any of those for very long yet, have you? I never thought we would have that many available, but they seem to be coming out of the woodwork."

"I don't know about that, but definitely a few are around. Maybe they feel a safety net is in place for them or something."

"I wondered that too," Terk muttered. "Anyway, what did you need for the job?"

Levi sighed. "Remember Kim?"

"Sure, and?"

"Her brother was traveling through Finland, and he's gone missing."

"Okay, and why do we think that's suspicious? He's a young single guy, right? Maybe he's just wandered off on his own for a while."

"He is all those things," Levi confirmed, "and you already figured that out. Wait, hang on a second, Terk." Levi took a moment for a side conversation. "What do you mean?" he asked someone on his end, and that was followed by some mumbling and bits and pieces of conversation that Terk couldn't quite catch.

Frowning as he listened, Terk followed a lifeline that came up against a blank wall. "*Huh.*"

"What *huh*?" Levi asked.

Ice popped into the phone conversation. "I'm here too, Terk. Is he alive?"

"That's ..." Terk stared at the blank wall. "He was, but I'm getting a blank wall right now. I'm not sure what that means."

At that, Cara looked over at him and explained, "If a lifeline hits a blank wall, it usually means a major injury, and he's in between life and death, but I'm not getting that same sense."

Terk extended a hand, and Cara and her sister Clary both grabbed on, their energies zapping through his system. He closed his eyes, feeling their combined energies working through this lifeline.

"We have a signature on him," Terk shared, "but something definitely is off at the other end."

"Yeah, and that's what this guy who contacted me was getting at."

"Explain."

"His name is Walker, and he told me that I needed to go deal with something in Finland. At the time, I didn't know anything about it. I felt as if he was almost pushing me in a way. He wants to work for me on this job, but I didn't have a job there. But then Kim came forward and said her brother was in Finland. So I wondered if it was related somehow, and that's when it came back that Kim hadn't been able to contact her brother at all."

Terk asked, "Levi, when you say Walker, did you mean Walker Habernack?"

"Yeah, do you know him?"

"Oh, I know him all right. He's got some pretty good precog abilities."

"But then why wouldn't he have known ahead of time?"

"He's likely contacting you because he's seen something down the road. What does Kim have for information?"

"Her brother went over to meet some special healer in Finland, and that's when he went missing."

Terk looked around the table, as they all stared at each other. Terk's gaze landed on Calum, who immediately nodded.

"I got this one."

"Levi, Calum will meet Walker in Finland. We'll need the details on Kim's brother and anything else you've got as soon as possible."

"You got it," Levi said, "and, Terk, Kim's family—"

"I know. That's not an issue. We'll pick up after this and see. Stay in touch. Calum will be on the way soon." After ending the call, he looked over at Calum. "You're sure?"

Calum nodded. "Absolutely. I'm in. When it comes to family, you know we're always there."

There was no arguing with that.

CHAPTER 1

W ALKER HABERNACK PULLED up on the side of the road and reached for the map sitting in the passenger seat. He was supposed to meet Calum in another hour, but, before he raced to the airport, he wanted a chance to check out a couple addresses he had in mind.

He needed some information before he went all-in. In his mind, in his heart, he wondered just what was going on here, but again, the frustration of not knowing much was evident. He just knew something bad was about to happen. Now, if only he were lucky enough to get there in time to stop it, that would be great. But this ugly sense inside him suggested that he was probably already too late.

However, as a precog, he knew that sense of foreboding came because he was aware of what one avenue in the future *could* be, yet wouldn't necessarily turn out that way. He still had time to change things.

He knew about Kim's brother at this point; he'd been filled in. Walker also understood that Levi was considering hiring Walker. It was supposed to be about getting his feet wet with the team, and this was a test job, but Walker also knew that wouldn't work. He hadn't told Terk that because, whatever was going on, regardless of the bells ringing in his ears, Walker needed to be there. If only he knew why, and, because he didn't know, he was very edgy and short-tempered.

He'd connected with Terkel, but Terk was not the easiest person to talk to either … by far. Walker almost laughed at that. If there were ever two peas in a pod, they were him and Terkel, but then probably a lot of psychics had a similar viewpoint.

Walker went way back with Terk. Even now Walker wanted something different in life and was trying to figure out how to find it. So, he was looking at Terk sideways, wondering how he'd made everything in his life suddenly happen. It was worth a long conversation, but Walker wasn't sure if Terkel would be open enough to share details. It was also possible that he would keep the information of how he'd pulled it off to himself.

Walker had also blocked the psychic door to stop Terkel from getting into his head. Terkel was one of those guys who generally would not force it, but, if he needed something, he wouldn't bother with niceties and then apologize afterward, which was okay in a true emergency. Still, Walker felt pressure that he didn't normally sense, and that made him uneasy right now.

Terkel would say that was all the more reason why Walker should be talking and keeping the doors open, letting everybody know that something was here, that something was happening, so that a bigger alert system would be in place, if and when it came to needing help.

Walker didn't know Calum but knew that he'd worked on Terkel's team when they worked with the CIA. The fact that Terkel had gone private was something Walker was still adjusting to, but maybe it went along with Terk having a woman in his life now. That was something most of them avoided on a long-term basis, just because it was too dangerous. Too much crap was going on in the world around them, and they couldn't really afford to have anybody tied up in it more than they were themselves.

Nobody wanted to deal with the outcome and all that pressure that came from having somebody else to look after. Even though in many cases, there was just no choice because you were already hooked into the relationship, into the emotions, and it was pretty darn hard to change it. And, if that happened to Terkel, Walker could understand it, except that Terkel was an old hand. That, in itself, told Walker that it had to be a very special woman to put Terkel on this pathway to have a family.

Walker heard the rumbling in the far recesses of his brain and shook his head. "No, Terk, not ready to talk to you yet." When that was followed by what Walker could only describe as a half laugh, he groaned, then opened up his mind after all. "What?" Walker barked.

Well now, that's better, Terkel replied easily. *I wanted to tell you that Calum's flight has been delayed by a good half hour.*

"I would have found that out when I checked the arrivals board," he muttered. "You didn't need to contact me for that."

No, but communication makes life a lot easier. How are you, by the way?

"Fine," he grumbled. "Or I will be if this damn urging will stop dragging me down this crazy pathway."

Terkel paused for a moment. *Sometimes we can do nothing but follow through on the messages we receive.*

"Doesn't mean I like it," Walker muttered.

No, I'm sure you don't, Terk agreed. *But, since I do know Kim, if this involves her brother, I'll thank you ahead of time for helping her out.*

Walker sighed. "The trouble is, I don't know who is involved. I never do. I just get these pieces of information, and I thought I was doing okay with that kind of scenario. I thought I could pick and choose what to act on. Then suddenly I get something like this, where I don't have a choice, and the messages go on and on," he complained, his tone snappy in the emptiness of the car.

Terkel chuckled. *Isn't that the truth? Just know you're not alone in that.*

"Again, that's all good, but it doesn't really help."

No, of course it doesn't, Terk noted. *You should feel better knowing that potentially something is out there for you that'll be a help.*

"No, not at all," Walker disagreed. "This isn't necessarily anything I want to do, and it's gotten worse."

Worse?

"Yes, worse, or maybe a better way to describe it is *stronger,* a little *wider.* It's one of the reasons I keep you butted out, until I can figure out what is really going on."

In my experience, I find that having people to talk to really helps. You can explain and explore the aspects of why that energy is changing, he pointed out, *but the biggest find we have come across ourselves, in my whole team, is that our severe injuries, triggered by a massive change, also created a shift in our abilities—stronger and wider,* he muttered, trying to put Walker's own point of view in perspective.

At that, Walker frowned. "Yeah, I did have something like that. I expected it to make things easier, not worse."

We're finding it makes things, Terk hesitated and then added, *different.*

"Yeah? That's a load of BS," Walker muttered. "*Different*

doesn't mean anything."

No, different means different, Terk stated, with a cheery tone. *Like in our case, … stronger. Some changes in the style of skills, some changes in the strength, and, because we're a large team, we have definitely seen growth in what we can do and how we can do it. If you had a team around, you would find the same thing.*

"It's a good thing I don't then, isn't it?" he stated easily.

Still fighting it, are you?

"It hasn't done me any good to fight it. However, if I thought it would help, I would be fighting it a whole lot harder."

Yeah, I haven't found that to work out so well myself, Terkel admitted. *And, if you had a team, you would find that your abilities would get a lot stronger and faster too.*

"Never been much of a team player," Walker muttered.

That's not so. You did great with a team in the navy.

"Yeah, right up until they didn't like what I could or couldn't do," he whispered harshly.

Got it, Terkel replied, his tone soft and clear. *The lack of ability to accept what we do, and the parameters under which we do it, often pisses people off more than helps anything,* he stated, taking a mild tone. *So that much, I do understand.*

Walker nodded. "What about Calum?"

He's strong and getting stronger all the time, Terkel shared. *He'll be a good one to have at your back.*

"I'm not used to having anybody at my back," Walker declared, with that same harsh anger again.

You can only play the lone wolf for so long, before some of this starts to eat away at you, Terkel noted. *Let Calum help you on this job and then talk to us afterward.*

"Won't change anything," he muttered.

If it doesn't, it doesn't. I'm not forcing you into anything, despite what your paranoia might suggest.

Walker groaned. "I didn't used to be paranoid."

No, and I think that comes on as a side effect of our abilities too, Terkel suggested, his tone gentle. *Nobody understands us quite like the rest of us.*

"And yet do they even understand?" Walker asked curiously. "I mean, how could they? Even though you're inside my head, you still don't know who I am, what I am, and how I'm operating."

No, but I can sure see an awful lot more of that now, Terkel admitted, with a chuckle. *I know you're operating very well, but you're kind of disconnected, as if you haven't fully integrated back from whatever injury you had going on in your world. Anyway, this is a discussion for another time. For now, just get to the airport and pick up Calum. He's a good guy, and he won't scare so easily.*

And, with that, Terkel was gone.

ASHLEY HENKELL SPUN around in a circle once again, looking for those unseen eyes that she knew were searching for her, hunting her, and yet she had no idea who it was, or why. She just instinctively knew that she was in danger, but that danger was coming from a direction she didn't understand. It was a source she didn't recognize, and that made her situation seem even more precarious.

She'd always avoided help from family and friends because nobody seemed to really understand who and what she was. As much as she tried to explain, her family never really got it, and now she was living in a more isolated situation than normal, waiting for this one man to show up for his appointment, but he was already two days late.

She knew something was wrong; she just didn't know what. It definitely had to do with her, and, while she didn't know why, it had given her an edginess that was hard to relax around.

Given the choice, she would be long gone. Maybe travel to the Maldives or to visit friends. Maybe do something crazy and go anyplace where millions of people would be, instead of this calm and almost isolated existence she currently found herself in. This had been her preferred existence, until the shit hit the fan, and she had become a target. Somehow, even though she didn't know any of the details, she'd become *the hunted*.

When she heard a vehicle drive slowly by, she stopped at the window and stared out, taking refuge behind the curtain. Nothing was outside, nothing that she could see, but she heard the vehicle slowly rumble on past her place.

She frowned at that, all her instincts telling her to run, to get out of the house, and to move. Then again, where would she go? Where would she run to? It was a wet and cloudy day out there. If the sun were out, and it was a bit warmer, she could certainly disappear into the woods for a few hours, but right now? If she went out and caught a cold and had no place to go, she would still have to come back and face whatever it was that had chased her away.

She didn't really have a safe room, something she would have sworn she didn't need—until now. *Now,* she could see a certain naïvety in her actions. Though, if she would have had any idea that she would experience this level of fear, she might have done things differently. Right now, all she could do was stay frozen in place and watch, knowing that the time was coming for whatever it was. She had no idea why or who, but it was charging toward her at an absolutely horrific pace.

When her phone rang not too long afterward, she stared down at it, recognizing McClintock's number. She quickly snatched it up and in the calmest tone she could manage, she answered, "Hello."

Almost instantly her old friend snapped, "What's the matter?"

"Nothing, just a bit edgy today."

After a moment of hard silence, he muttered, "That's exactly why you shouldn't be living out there."

"And yet, for all of a lifetime up until now, it's been perfectly fine," she stated. "I'm just not sure what's wrong with today."

"That's why I'm calling. It seems something is wrong in the world."

"Something is *always* wrong in the world," she argued, refusing to give in to that philosophy. "Plus, you and I both know that, if something is after me, it'll get here, and not a whole lot I can do about it."

"That's not true," he argued, his tone sharp. "It's still up to you to look after yourself and to keep yourself safe from whatever it is that makes so much trouble in the world."

"Yeah, but don't we sound like a couple of crazy loons," she muttered. "I couldn't begin to tell you what is wrong. I just have this weird edginess."

"I couldn't tell you what is wrong either," he snapped, "but I'm calling nonetheless."

She smiled at that. "I appreciate it. Really I do, and you know that. Honestly, it hasn't been an easy time for you, and I know that you don't really have anything else to think about but crap stuff right now. So the fact that you realize something's going on in my world is really appreciated."

He snorted. "That's a load of holy crock," he muttered. "You know perfectly well that, if I could do something to fix this, I would be there in a heartbeat."

"I presume that means that you can't then," she questioned, "fix it, I mean."

"No, I can't. I just don't know why I see men coming though."

She winced. "Yeah, I saw that too, … but I don't know why. I don't know who they are or where they are coming from."

He chuckled. "That just adds to the confusion, doesn't it?"

"Yes, it absolutely does," she agreed. "It would be a whole lot easier if I had some way to know just what was going on, but it's not as if we ever get those kinds of answers."

"No, and believe me, I've looked," McClintock stated. "I know my abilities are nowhere near what they used to be, but I'm not getting answers, and that concerns me. I always expect, when I reach out in your direction, that I'll find peace and tranquility. Yet, when I reached out today, I got the exact opposite."

"You know, it could just be me," she suggested, with a sigh. "I don't understand why I'm edgy or what the hell is going on, but rest assured that I'm working to control it."

"Maybe instead of trying to control it, you should lean into it. Slide into that feeling and sort out what's happening, so maybe we can both get some rest."

She snorted. "You can get rest anytime."

"Yeah, and, if something happens to you," he snapped,

"how will that make me feel?"

"You've done what you can do by warning me," she told him gently, "so the rest will be whatever it'll be."

"Don't talk like that," he declared. "I hate it when you get fatalistic."

She sighed. "I don't really know any other way to be."

"You could though, if you wanted to," he snapped. "You could come in and be with people again."

"I've spent a long time on my own," she shared.

"That's been your choice," he muttered, "but you don't have to stay out there."

"No, I don't. However, sometimes it just feels that I don't really have another option."

"And that is all gibberish from your own head," he muttered. "Anyway, I can't stay on the phone. You know what you have to do," he said, and, with that, he ended the call.

She looked down at the phone, wondering if he really meant to say it in that way, because she really didn't know what she *had to do*. She just knew that something was shifting, and, while she didn't know in what direction, she suspected it would come to a head very, very soon.

With that thought in her consciousness, she looked around and quickly gathered her wallet, checking to be sure she had her ID, some cash, and credit cards, then stuffed it into her pocket. Grabbing her hiking boots and a good walking coat and stick, she stepped out the door.

She didn't know what she was running from, but something out there was coming her way, and she wasn't at all sure she wanted to meet up with them just yet.

CHAPTER 2

ASHLEY HAD BEEN outside for an hour, walking the fields and seeking the peace and quiet that had been so elusive all day. When she realized that home was her logical next stop, she turned and headed steadily back in the direction of her small house. As she came across the road, intent on walking a slightly smoother return path, a vehicle drove past, with two men seated in the front.

She frowned at the energy, but the vehicle went by too quickly for her to see anything, yet something was there. She pondered who they were and watched as they pulled into the turnoff that would take them to her road. By watching across the field, she saw them head in a steady and relentless path to her home.

Sure enough, they pulled up out front.

She froze out in the field, wondering whether she should be heading in to talk to them or not, only to realize that it wouldn't make much difference, since these men would just keep coming back until she did. She had no idea who they were or what drove them, but something did. … Something was odd about one of them too.

No.

She froze at that correction and shook her head. No, something was odd about both of them. They were both the odd ones out in a way. Yet they were together. She picked up the pace, and, as one of men stepped back after knocking on her door, she called out to them. One of the men lifted a hand in acknowledgment, so she slowed her pace, until she walked right up to them.

As she got closer to her house, she watched their energy, studying it, looking for that danger she'd been sensing, yet finding nothing of the sort. That worried her more than anything. She was expecting them to be the reason for her unease, and yet they seemed ... She didn't want to say *harmless* because nothing was harmless about them. They were both incredibly powerful men. However, she didn't even know if they understood just how much power they were wielding in a subconscious way.

One of them did seem to be awfully sure of himself. She wasn't so sure about the other one. He just glared at her, as if wanting to be anywhere else.

She sighed, as she looked at him. "So, what's this one? Another unwilling psychic?"

He froze at that, and the other man rumbled with laughter.

She smiled at the friendly one. "I'm Ashley. Who are you?"

He looked at her and in a gentle tone replied, "I'm Calum. Nice to meet you."

She looked back at the other man and nodded at him, trying an easing tone with him this time. "I suppose I shouldn't piss you off right from the beginning."

He shrugged. "You spoke the truth. I can hardly argue with that."

"That's a step forward," she muttered, as she opened up the door to her small home and let them in. "Do you want to explain why you've come?" She dug right in, thinking there was no need to beat around the bush.

"You mean, you can't tell?" Calum asked, with a note of amusement.

She turned to him and replied, "I can tell some things, but that's not exactly where I like to spend my energy. I'm a healer. My energy is reserved for that."

"That's exactly why we're here." The second man spoke this time. "I am Walker, and we're looking for somebody who's gone missing."

She studied him and then knew right away. "Oh, Frank, of course. He was due in two days ago and never showed up. I don't know him personally, and I didn't know if it was maybe a case of cold feet on his part."

"That would be one possible explanation," Calum agreed, with a nod. "His sister is worried."

At that, Ashley sighed. "I hope you don't mind if I put on the teakettle." Then she walked over to her kitchen, just a small area that was more than enough for her, but, with these two huge men in her house, it seemed not nearly enough, and suddenly her space looked too small. The one with angst in his temperament was looking at her with an odd expression.

She refused to acknowledge the energy arcing between them. She'd felt that once before, and, up until now, no good had come of it. She couldn't understand why he was even here to begin with, when it was so obvious he didn't want to be. She put on the teakettle, then turned to look at Walker. "Do you know either of them, the brother or the sister?"

He frowned and shook his head. "No."

"So, why are you here?" she asked, her tone crisp and direct. "If you don't know them, what brings you?" He glanced over at Calum, as if for an answer, but Calum just waited, letting Walker either dig his own grave or answer the question in a way that would make sense.

Walker sighed. "Obviously you work with energy, so maybe you'll understand when I say that I was driven to tell somebody about a problem over here," he shared. "Now, if you're asking for more information than that, I don't really have it to give."

"And it's this young man who's the problem?"

"He has become a problem," Walker clarified. "I don't know for sure. I just know that, when I contacted Levi, who is the sister's boss, he put me in touch with Terkel, who sent Calum here over with me to sort it out."

"So, you both made the trip on the assumption that something was wrong. Yet you have nothing to back it up?" She made the statement as if it were commonplace to have such a scenario, but she was astonished in a very pleasant way. Very few people cared about others enough to inconvenience themselves like that on a hunch, particularly when they didn't even know the whole story.

"Something like that, yes," Calum confirmed, with a smile. "You know, Terkel would understand."

She stared at him and nodded. "Terkel? You mentioned him before." Then she thought about it. "Like six feet tall, kind of raspy tone, a little bit cranky, very standoffish, and never wrong? Terkel, *huh*?"

At that, Calum laughed and laughed. "I really wish he could hear that description of himself, but, yes, that's Terkel to a tee."

She glared at him and then called out to the room around them. "Terkel, what are you up to?"

Both Calum and Walker looked at her in astonishment,

but then came an odd *clap* like thunder, followed by an energy buzz in the room.

She looked over at her visitors. "Presumably you guys can't project yourselves, so I'll need to assist you in this conversation." Then she turned around and yelled again, "Terkel, if you can show yourself, now would be the time to do it. It'll be a lot easier for everybody involved."

A sudden shimmer appeared in the room.

Ashley laughed. "You're getting stronger. Good for you."

Terkel's tone rippled through the room, but it was a little more tired and definitely frustrated. "It would be really nice if you didn't make life so difficult all the time."

"Yeah? Well, it would be really nice if you didn't make the life of other people so difficult all the time," she snapped right back.

"For a healer, you've got to be one of the most irritating people I've ever met," Terk muttered.

"Likewise," she replied. "So these men came from you?"

"More or less, yes," he confirmed. "Calum works for me. He's part of the same team I worked with before at the CIA, only we're private now."

At that, one of her eyebrows shot up, but Ashley didn't say anything, not wanting to interrupt the flow of information.

"The grumpy gentleman, that would be Walker, contacted a friend of ours over a problem in Finland. As soon as we realized that Kim's brother had gone to see a specialized healer, I determined it was probably you and sent them there."

"Yet, from the looks on their faces, neither of them realized you know who I am."

"I didn't exactly fill them in on that because, of course, I didn't want them prejudging the situation."

"No, but prejudging is not the same thing as providing them with complete information," Ashley clarified smoothly. Speaking as somebody who had worked for the government until she couldn't stomach it any longer, she continued. "You and I both know the truth of that."

"Absolutely, and I will make my peace with them later," Terk admitted smoothly. "In the meantime, we are trying to locate Kim's brother."

"If you're talking about Frank, as I told your men, he was due to come in and see me two days ago, but he never showed." A sense of consternation filled the air, and she nodded. "It's not the first time it's happened with one of my clients," she shared, a bit of false calm settling in. "A lot of people get cold feet when they realize what they're coming to, and, if he hadn't been warned ahead of time, it would be even harder on him."

Terk added, "I don't know him and wasn't aware that he was headed there, so I highly doubt he would have listened to me."

"And yet you," she said in a mocking tone, "have never been known for being subtle, so I'm surprised there would even be a question about it now."

"If I do manage to get my hands on him," Terk replied, "I'll try to explain the situation a little bit better, but he didn't ask for information. Nobody came to me, and unfortunately nobody from Levi's side even had a glimmer of what was happening either. I just knew at the mention of a special healer in Finland that it would be you."

"Thanks for that at least. I'll talk to you later." And, with a wave of her hand, Terkel disappeared.

When she turned and looked at the other two, she saw

that both were beyond disconcerted. She nodded. "So, what is this really about?"

SEEING HER ENERGY lifeline intertwining with his, Walker was distracted and frowned at her, also not exactly sure how to proceed on locating Frank. "We're trying to find this young man," he repeated, "and I admit you're the only person I know who can arrange energy quite like that."

At that, Calum started laughing again and spoke to Ashley. "Don't mind my rudeness, but you're the only one I've ever seen dismiss Terk like that."

She shrugged. "We've known each other a long time," she shared comfortably, and then she stopped and tilted her head to the side, a bit shocked. "Good God, he's about to become a father?"

At that, Calum grinned, the smile splitting his face. "Yeah, he sure is."

"And twins at that," she muttered, with a smile. "Will wonders never cease? This is a day."

"Now that we have a better understanding of who we all are," Calum noted, "can you help us locate this young man?"

She looked at him and shrugged. "I don't know anything about him, really. As I've mentioned, twice now, Frank was due to arrive a few days ago for a healing session, but he didn't show. That doesn't mean a whole lot in my world because a lot of people don't show up, even when they're supposed to. They get cold feet, don't realize what they're up against, somebody talks them out of it, or whatever. All kinds of scenarios can happen."

Calum nodded. "I get that, but I was hoping you might

have an idea of his planned itinerary, of how he was traveling, where he was coming from, things along that line."

She pondered that, then walked over to a small desk and picked up an appointment book. "He was coming from the US. He was flying out of Texas, as far as I know, and was due in two days ago. I offered to let him stay in my guest cabin because, when I'm doing a ton of work on somebody, it's often too hard for them to leave for a day or so. They're too exhausted," she murmured. "And, if that's the case, I don't really want them driving around. He could pick up a rental car at the airport and should have been here days ago," she explained, with a shrug, pointing out the appointment listed in her book.

Walker took the book from her, checked it gently, flipped back a couple months and noted, "You're not exactly booked up."

"No, I'm sure not," she agreed, taking the book from his hands. "Can't say I have a preference for killing myself in that line again." When he looked at her, she shrugged. "You'll have to ask Terkel about that," she muttered. "I don't exactly have a great history with people in this business. I only help those who make their way to me."

"Why is that?" Walker asked.

"Because I believe that they are the ones I'm supposed to help," she stated simply. "If I advertise or do anything along that line, it would be a never-ending circus of people, including journalists, medical professionals, and various other whatnots. None of which I want in my world, nor am I prepared to deal with them."

Calum smiled. "That is very understandable. As somebody who was dragged into all this, dealt with the CIA and the rest of the government, side by side with Terkel, I understand how ugly things can get. I'm sorry for the experiences you've had, but, if you're waiting for people who are in need to come to you," he suggested, "surely you would have gone looking for this young man when he didn't show up."

She looked at him, then smiled. "Not necessarily. He isn't exactly lost. He's just not here at my door."

"Ah." Calum nodded. "I suppose that makes a difference."

"Of course it makes a difference," she declared. "He could have been in town, or he could even be there now, still second-guessing himself."

"Do people really get that much in the way of themselves over this?" Walker asked curiously.

She nodded. "An awful lot of people don't really understand what I do and why I do it. So then, when they come, they are hesitant about what I have to tell them."

"How is your success rate?" Calum asked.

She looked at him, and Walker could see the confusion in her eyes. "What do you mean?" she asked, clearly not seeing where he was coming from.

Calum shrugged. "We have some pretty phenomenal healers working with Terkel now. I just wondered …" Then he stopped, realizing expressing his whole thought probably would sound insulting.

"You wondered how I stack up against them?" she asked, with a note of amusement. "Believe me. Clary and Cara don't give a crap."

His eyebrows shot up. "No, I don't imagine they would. You know them, do you?"

"I know them as healers on the ethers," she murmured. "We all work the same highways, the same energy. I've even been known to assist at certain times, mostly anonymously, just because I really don't want to interfere in anything going on in their space."

At that, he let out a silent whistle. "Do they have any idea?"

"That I'm helping? Of course," she stated, "but that doesn't mean they're acknowledging it though. In that situation, if they need help from someone like me, there isn't much time or energy for idle chatter."

"That makes sense, I guess. I don't really know that much about it myself."

"I suspect they don't really talk much about what we do because, … let's face it, not many people get it."

"No, you're right there," Calum said. "We've seen them do some pretty phenomenal things when healing us, as the last year has been extremely hard on all of us, including Terk. So you might want to cut Terkel a bit of slack."

She snorted at that. "Terkel wouldn't even thank me if I did, so the answer to that is *hell no*."

He burst out laughing. "Okay, it sounds like you really do know Terk and his team."

"I do," she declared. "*Of* them, anyway. I know people like them, and, whether you are the same or not, I don't know. However, I've had more than enough of government interference, government issues, bureaucracy, dictators, orders I didn't like, couldn't follow, and fought against. I watched the wrong people die and the wrong people rise to power. So, I really am not interested in having anything to do with that at all."

"You won't get an argument from me on that," Walker added. "Terk's team and I feel the same way."

She turned and looked at him. "Do you?"

"I do," he stated, his tone sincere, as he studied her. "You want to live in a world where you want to trust people, but, in your heart of hearts, you can't. Still, that doesn't mean you can't heal at that same level. My understanding is that anybody who is a healer has to work from love, has to work from that special level of understanding the true value of life, not from anger. So there has to be a way for you to find that special connection in order to do what you do."

She nodded. "You're right, which is also why I pick and choose my clients very carefully," she replied. "In this case, I was willing to take on Frank because he was so desperate and because everybody else had given up on him."

Calum stiffened. "We never heard anything about what was wrong with him."

"No, and he didn't tell his sister either," Ashley shared, "so nobody on that side of his life knows."

Calum nodded. "Oh, man, being alone and facing some sort of major health crisis is not easy. That's rough."

"It's not only difficult," she noted sadly, "but, in his case, it's likely to be fatal."

"But he's young," Calum argued.

"He's twenty-eight," Ashley stated simply, "which is old enough, but when it comes to losing what's important in life, you can bet it won't be old enough at all."

"I feel bad for Kim though," Calum murmured. "She has no idea."

"That's the way Frank wanted it. He wanted to either live or die his way through this, but to not have everybody be sad and angry because of what's happening," she explained.

Walker added, "As much as I understand that, people care about him, love him, and, if it's possible to save him, it would be nice to know it could happen."

"It's possible, but he needed to be here."

"You're using the past tense," Calum stated sharply.

She looked at him and nodded. "Unconsciously."

"You and I both know that even saying that *unconsciously* is bad news."

"I used it unconsciously because he's not here," she clarified. "I'm not saying he's dead. That is not the vibration I'm getting."

Calum relaxed slightly. "I sure hope you're right about that. Kim is quite worried about him."

ASHLEY STARED OFF in the distance, then nodded. "I'll have some tea, while I think about this." When the men shared a look, she nodded. "You are welcome to have tea with me, or you can leave. I really don't care."

Walker snorted. "Decided to take a page from my book, *huh?*"

She gave him a small smile. "Sometimes you use anger, ignorance, or just plain bad manners to chase people away," she noted, looking amused. "I try not to, but somehow it's just easier that way."

"It's easier, but it's also not fair to those around us."

At that, she laughed. "As if you're one to talk."

"I know. You're right," Walker admitted, his tone steady. "I definitely haven't been the easiest to live with, but that doesn't mean I would send people packing who needed my help."

"I don't know what it is you want from me," Ashley replied. "You'll have to go out and find Frank. If you bring him to me, I'll help him because he came to my door.

However, if you can't bring him to me, I can't do anything to help."

"Are you sure about that?" Calum asked gently.

She looked at him and then nodded. "I'm not a seeker. I'm not a hunter. I'm a healer. So, if and when you bring me somebody to heal, I'll do my best. Other than that, you're on your own."

She knew they didn't like what she had to say, but it's not as if she was making things up. These were just the facts of life, and they had to realize she could do only so much. If they brought Frank to her, she would do everything she could to help this young man, but something else was around Frank, and she didn't like it.

As the men went to leave, she called after them. "I don't know what this is worth because it's not my field, but I definitely sense ..." She pondered what she would say next. "I almost want to say *danger* around him."

"What kind of danger?" Calum asked, studying her carefully.

She looked over at him, trying to think of how to say it. "It's not easy to say, but ..." She hesitated and then let it slide. "I see two men with him, and I'm not sure who these men are, but they're not happy. It's almost as if maybe Frank saw something he wasn't supposed to see. I don't know. But I also get the feeling that Frank made it most of the way here, and now I have a sense on his part that he's—"

"Lost," Walker filled in. "I'm picking that up too."

She faced him and shrugged. "He isn't. Lost, that is. At least, not yet. If you can get him to me then ..." She let her tone trail off.

Walker glanced at Calum, and the two men nodded at her and stepped out onto her front porch.

They stood there talking, while she sipped her tea. They obviously didn't know that she could hear them fairly clearly, but they would be reporting to Terkel within seconds, and she knew that would stir the pot because Terkel knew about a lot of her abilities, if not all of them.

When her phone rang just minutes later, she answered it, looking out the window to see the two men driving away. "Now what, Terkel?"

"I need you to give me anything you have on this young man."

"I already gave it to your men, who are just now driving away," she stated, feeling that same fatigue settling deep inside.

"You can't save the world, you know?"

She laughed. "Which is why I'm living on the edge of the world, away from it all, away from that nightmare called war, called government, called whatever you want to call it," she shared. "I did that for as long as I could, for as long as I was forced to, until I could bargain my way out of there, and now I'm hidden with good reason. So they can't find me. Remember? The fact that your guys arrived on my doorstep doesn't make me happy."

"You can't hide forever," Terk said gently. "You can come join us here. We could protect you."

She gave a broken laugh. "You might protect me," she whispered, "but so much more is wrong with me that I don't think anybody can help."

"You're wrong about that, you know?" he countered, his tone gentle. "I'm so glad you're still alive."

"I'm alive, and you and I both know there's an ongoing scenario."

"Yet you haven't done anything about it," Terk noted, a

bit more harshly than he intended, "and, for that, I'm also grateful."

She felt the tears welling up in the back of her eyes. "I'm glad you think so," she muttered. "Some days are good, and then there are the rest."

"I think that's true for everybody."

"And yet," she replied, her tone smiling now, "you have twins on the way."

He chuckled. "I do, and, no, I had no idea that would ever be a part of my world. I could never have imagined this would be my new normal."

"I'm really glad for you. You deserve it. You're one of the good guys, Terkel, and, if you can find this young man, I told your men that I would do the best I could. I'm just … I'm not sure that anything can be done, particularly at this stage. Frank was already at a critical juncture prior to all this. So the sooner somebody brings him to me, the better."

"What about Clary and Cara?" he asked. "Calum mentioned something about you knowing them?"

"You should ask them," she suggested, with a laugh. "Maybe they don't know me, or maybe they don't want to acknowledge that they know me. Remember? When you're broken, most people jump ship and ignore the fact that you ever existed."

"I do know that," he countered, "but I've never been one for jumping ship. Just like McClintock too. Plus, I wouldn't know how to start. Still, I would need one hell of a big ship anyway because I always insist that my friends come with me. Remember that."

With that, he rang off, leaving her with tears streaming down her cheeks.

IN THE VEHICLE, heading back to the nearest town, Calum looked over at Walker. "What do you think?"

"Ashley's broken yet doesn't quite realize that she's essentially healed again," he replied.

Startled, Calum looked over at him. "That's not quite what I meant."

"You asked, and that's what I got."

"I think you're right though. She's been living out here on her own for so long that she doesn't realize how, in many ways, she doesn't need to anymore. She doesn't want to know," he stated.

"Her world was torn apart by whatever happened, and she's still … I won't say *fighting* it, but she isn't exactly free and clear about acknowledging that she has healed. She's still trying to get away from anybody who might be trying to get her to do something she doesn't want to do."

"It's a scary world out there when you're like us," Calum admitted. "If I hadn't had Terkel all these years, I don't know how well I would have done."

Surprised, Walker looked at him. "The fact that you have Terkel is huge."

"It really is, and I know a lot of people don't really get that, but he's been instrumental in pulling us all together, especially after our own government went after us." He quickly shared a shortened version of that story, and, when he was finished, Walker was stunned.

"Good God," Walker swore softly. "You would think they would learn."

"Nope, not only do they *not* learn, they don't care to learn. They're just out for themselves, ensuring that their butts are covered. It makes no difference to them about anybody else, and that's where the problem comes in. All of us have had our problems and issues with the government, but none of us ever dreamed they would try to take us all out like that."

"Is it over now?"

"It is, thank God. Now we're set up in a castle, like a real castle, in the outskirts of Manchester. I've got to tell you that it's one of the coolest places to live that you could ever imagine."

"Only if you've updated the plumbing and electrical," Walker quipped, laughing.

"No kidding. Plus, it comes with a bunch of properties with houses out on the land itself and whatnot."

"You're thinking about Ashley, aren't you?"

Calum shrugged. "Just something that I know from personal experience. When you're out in the cold, it's very hard to believe in anything and anyone else. But then, when you find out you have a team who cares and who can help, but will also keep their distance and not crowd you, it's life-changing."

Walker frowned at him, and Calum laughed. "Yeah, and you too," he added. "I know that she would be better off there with us, and I highly suspect that you would thrive there as well."

"What if I didn't?"

"Then you could leave," Calum offered. "Terk's team is not the government. Nobody is forcing anybody to do anything. You could stay or go. When you find yourself around a group of like-minded people who care and who have some of the same issues as you, it's a real game-changer."

"Maybe," Walker muttered. "Not sure I'm ready for something like that, though it sounds like a commune or something."

"Yeah, I get that. To a certain extent, we were all hesitant on that aspect as well," he shared, "not only living with each other but knowing our special energy-working skills. However, we don't intrude on the others in our team. We set up those rules to respect each other. Even now, with all the babies coming at probably the same time, having all these built-in babysitters will be a boon, plus the babies will thrive in an environment where they all belong. So, yeah, even with any expected drawbacks, it's all worked out way better than any of us could have imagined. I mean, it wasn't exactly what any of us were looking for, but trust Terkel to know what we needed," he shared, taking on a serious tone, "and that's the big difference. We trusted him, and the big guy didn't let us down."

Such affection filled his tone that Walker was surprised. Then again after this talk about babies... maybe nothing about this group would surprise him again. "I know he appears to always have a lot of supporters around him. That in itself is admirable."

"Terkel doesn't give a crap about *admirable*," Calum stated cheerfully. "That's not his style, but he does care about his people and what they are up to and whether they're doing the right thing for themselves or not." Calum laughed. "I don't even know what he would say about you, but I do know that he worries about you, and that would be Terkel all over again." Calum sighed.

"He doesn't need to worry. You know that, right?"

"Sure, and I could tell him that until I'm blue in the face. It won't make a damn bit of difference," he replied cheerfully.

And that was something else that Walker knew was true. "Damn," he muttered.

"No pressure, none at all," Calum murmured but then chuckled. "I'm just telling you that, if you ever want to have a place to come in out of the cold, we have a spot for you."

"Is that what it'll be, a collective for misfits?" he asked suddenly.

"I'm not sure about the misfit part because it certainly seems like everybody there functions pretty highly and couldn't be pegged as a misfit. Yet we all needed a home, a safe place, and, I think, in that sense, what we're doing is very valuable."

"Maybe so," Walker conceded, "but it still sounds like a wayward house for lost and lonely psychics."

Calum burst out laughing. "I can see how you could look at it that way and even get a little offended," he admitted, with another chuckle, "but I'm sure you know very well how few people out there will even have anything to do with us because of the things we can do. I mean, if you know that somebody can read your mind, would you want them in your house?"

At that, Walker felt his own psychic doors slamming shut, and Calum burst out laughing again. "Hey, I don't read minds," he pointed out, "so you're safe. For now."

"Yeah, says you," Walker muttered. "It's still pretty unnerving to have Terkel walking through my brain all the time."

"Yeah, until you realize why he's doing it and how much faster and easier it is on all of us sometimes."

"Yeah, in what way?"

"If anything is wrong with my son or my wife, wherever

I am in the world, you can bet that I know Terkel's got my back. Plus, he has healers there to help us get through whatever it is that needs to be gotten through. And, just like that, the rest of the team comes together. ... I think of us as brothers in a way. Now brothers *and* sisters. We've all been to hell and back already, but we're still there because we care. I give full kudos to Terkel for having us all live together there," he stated. "Especially now that we have families. In the meantime, we have to find this young man. I think, in his own way, Frank may feel like the world has walked away from him and left him out in the cold."

At the nearest small town, they stopped in at the local motel and booked a room for the night. As they were checking in, Calum pulled out a picture of Kim's brother and asked the woman at the front desk if she'd seen him.

She looked at the photo, then shook her head. "No," she said initially, but then she frowned and looked at the picture again. "Maybe, but he didn't look that good."

"He's sick. He came here to see Ashley."

Her eyes widened, and she drew a cross over her chest, but she nodded quickly. "Then that could have been him. He asked for a room, and I was getting it for him, but then he got called outside by somebody he seemed to know. As I recall, he went out and then came back to cancel the room because he already had a place to stay." She shrugged. "The next thing I knew, he was gone."

"Did you see who he talked to?"

She shook her head. "No, I didn't see the man—or anyone for that matter. It was a black car, but that's all I have for you," she replied apologetically.

"Thank you," Calum said, with a smile, and she relaxed at that. He quickly paid for their room for the night and got the key.

As they got up to the room, Walker nodded with relief that two big beds were there for them. "I was afraid that, in a small place like this motel, we would end up in the same bed."

"If that's what happened, we would have made it work," Calum stated. "One of us could have hit the floor if it was a problem. We'll probably wind up on different shifts anyway."

"True enough," Walker muttered. "What do you think about what the desk clerk said?"

"Sounds like Frank knew somebody, although he wasn't expecting to meet anyone. I'm not sure whether that was a friend of his or what. Who knows? Maybe he did know somebody here." Calum pulled out his phone. "I'm sending a text to Levi to have him grill Kim a little. We need to find out who Frank might have had for friends, here and elsewhere. And how did he find out about Ashley? The fact that he was willing to make the trip over here to see her is interesting in itself. His even knowing about her is also on the odd side."

"Why is it odd?"

"She only accepts so many people, and the ones who make their way to her have heard from someone else she had already treated or knew. How does anybody find her?"

"I'm sure she would say that's the psychic part again, and, if you were somebody she could help, you would get there, and, if you weren't somebody she could help, then you wouldn't."

"That could be exactly what's going on, but let's find out if any friends of Frank had come here before him." They quickly unpacked, and, just as they were heading out to find something to eat, Levi contacted them with the answers.

"No known friends in Finland."

"*Great*," Walker muttered.

Levi continued. "Nobody Kim knows of over there knew Frank was coming, but that doesn't mean he didn't tell people. That is a whole different story. Just because Kim knew nothing doesn't mean Frank didn't tell a half-dozen other people."

"Exactly," Walker agreed. "The question is, who would he have told? And even though he may well have told people, what difference does it make?"

"Would they have come over here to see him?" Calum asked. "Maybe they wanted to persuade him not to go see this crazy healer, you know? I mean, maybe they really loved and believed him but were terrified of what some backwoods healer might do. There could be all kinds of scenarios like that."

Soon they headed into a small café, sat down, then ordered dinner while they discussed the case. By the time the food arrived, they were more than ready to eat and tucked into it quickly. As they sat here afterward, sipping coffee, Walker murmured, "Ashley's very unique."

Calum looked at him and smiled. "She is, indeed. She's also fairly gifted."

"Yeah, I'll talk to Terkel about what she mentioned about the two healer women."

"I'm sure they're all discussing it right now." Calum laughed. "Particularly if the twins knew she was there in prior healings but hadn't really been aware of her presence."

"Ashley didn't seem all that unusual when we were there," Walker noted, "so I'm not really sure how I feel about that. But I also presume some energy was flying around that room that we couldn't really see or feel. Not me at least. Did you feel it?"

"No, I didn't," Calum replied, "but I think she had everything pulled in tight against her, that protectiveness again."

"Of course all that does is make you want to find out what happened to her."

"Exactly."

Just then a bent-over old man walked up to their table, looking at them with a sharp eye. "You were at Ashley's."

They both nodded. "We were," Calum replied, with a smile, and he motioned at the empty seat. "Did you want to join us?"

The other man hesitated. "What do you want with her?"

Walker realized that concern for Ashley had brought him over. He smiled at the older gentleman and shared, "She was due to have somebody come to … her. He made the appointment but didn't show up. That young man is the brother of a friend of ours, and we believe he's gone missing."

At that, the older man's eyes widened, and he stared at them for a very long time. Finally he nodded. "Weird things happen here," he shared cautiously.

"They can happen anywhere," Walker stated, "but that weirdness comes from people, not from just places."

The old man chuckled. "Isn't that the truth," he muttered. "I don't want anything to happen to her."

"I get it," Walker confirmed. "We're not here to hurt her."

Again came that same intense look, and then he nodded. "See that you don't." With that, he slowly moved off to the door.

Walker wanted to run after him and ask for details on

Ashley, but knowing that the man was here to support Ashley and to look after her also meant that he wouldn't likely spill the private details Walker was curious to know about. Better that he asked her directly. Whether she answered him or not would be a different story, but at least he would have made an honest attempt to get to the truth.

They paid for their dinner, got up, and walked outside, but no sooner had they headed in the direction of the motel, Calum spoke up. "We've got a tail."

"Yeah, on the left, two men," Walker muttered.

"I see just one," Calum admitted, glancing at Walker.

Walker added, "The other one is farther behind. If you see the energy trail, a thread connects the two of them."

Calum pondered that for a minute. "Interesting. I can't see the energy trail at all."

"Trust me. They're both there, and they're connected."

"I thought you were a precog?"

"I am, though I don't generally tell people because the whole business of precogs tends to be kind of a crap show," he muttered. "I might be right today, and I might be wrong tomorrow."

"You were right about Frank."

"Maybe, maybe not," Walker muttered. "It's really too early to tell."

"No, not at all. We can tell already that we have a problem on our hands. So now it's just a matter of figuring out the details."

"Well," Walker added, "I hope Kim's okay with the details being a bit sketchy at the moment because I highly suspect that this tail will want to talk to us but probably has no knowledge to share."

"Yeah, you think?"

"Yep, considering the way they're moving up on us. Plus, they'll just be the local hired thugs."

"How do you want to play it?" Calum asked.

"Good question." Walker sighed. "Personally, I'm all about just busting it wide open and asking what the hell they want."

"Sounds good to me." Calum laughed. "If nothing else it would give us a good idea who they are. By the time we brace them, they'll either be aggressive as hell or proclaiming their innocence. My vote is they'll pretend to be innocent."

"Let's find out, shall we?" Walker asked. "We'll just confront them then and see what we've got." With that he looked over at Calum and added, "I'll grab this closest guy in three, two, one." With that, Walker turned on the spot and quickly snatched the man behind him and pinned him against the wall around the corner.

The stranger didn't even have a chance to open his mouth, and he stood, glaring at him.

"Why are you following us?" Walker asked, his tone hard.

The man looked at him and in guttural English tried to play it cool. "Not following."

"Yes, you are," Walker stated.

The man shook his head several times.

Walker stepped back to study him and decided to go all-in. "Did you have something to do with that young man's disappearance?"

The stranger glared at him, starting to lose some of that innocence, but again shook his head.

At that giveaway, Walker smiled. "We'll just see what your partner has to say about that."

"No partner," he said.

"Yeah? I don't believe you," Walker replied.

Just then Calum came around the corner, pushing a second man, who was protesting at the rough handling. When he saw his partner, he subsided. "Now that we have both of you here," Calum announced, his tone threatening, "I suggest you start talking."

The second man sneered at him. "Why should we?"

"Because we're looking for that young man," Walker replied, raising his voice, "and we're not going anywhere until we find him."

At that, the first man started to get nervous and mumbled something. The second one turned to him and yelled, "Shut up."

"I didn't have anything to do with that," the first guy wailed. "Honest."

"I don't expect much in the way of honesty from scum like you," Walker stated, glaring at him. "Now tell me what happened to that young man."

"Nothing," the first guy said, "at least, nothing I know about." He turned and looked at his partner, who was now openly glaring at him.

"Sounds like you two are on a different venture here," Walker noted.

"No, no, not at all," the talkative first guy argued. "I don't know what the problem is."

But his partner still glared at him.

Walker pointed to his partner. "Apparently he does, and he's just not willing to talk."

The first man started to say something but then fell silent.

Calum looked over at Walker. "Sounds like we need the local authorities."

"Yep," he muttered. He stepped back to pull out his phone.

The first man wailed, "Wait. You don't understand. I can't have the law involved."

"What do I care?" Walker asked. "You're following strangers in town, so you obviously knew you were heading for this. What difference does it make to me if the law picks you up and takes you in for a little talk?"

"Of course we'll want to find someone who's honest and clear in this town, which will take a little bit, I would guess," Calum noted. "We'll probably talk to a few of them, but we are bound to find at least one, right?"

At that, the first man, his Adam's apple in his throat bobbing up and down nervously, muttered, "I didn't have anything to do with the guy disappearing."

"So why are you following us?" Walker asked.

He shrugged. "I was hired. They gave me a couple hundred dollar bills to keep track of where you went."

"Now we need to know who that was, how they contacted you, and how I can contact them," Calum declared in a less-than-pleasant tone.

The talkative first guy shook his head. "No, no, no, it doesn't work that way. I won't get paid if you contact them."

"Sounds to me as if you won't get paid at all if your partner here has his say because he'll just turn you in for giving him up to the law." Walker turned and looked at the second man, who was still glaring, and then Walker laughed. "Yeah, he knows the score. The missing guy is young, and he doesn't really understand what this is all about. But you do, don't you?" Walker asked the silent guy.

Now the second guy spoke. "That's interesting news to me. You don't know what you're talking about. None of this is a problem."

Walker frowned. "Maybe not for you, but it might be for somebody else, particularly if people are looking for somebody who's gone missing."

"I don't know anything about the young man," the second guy repeated. "We were just hired to watch you guys. You're strangers, and nobody trusts strangers around these parts."

"Now nobody will hire the two of you to watch strangers for no reason either," Walker stated, glaring at him. "I really don't give a shit, so we can just call the local LEOs and let them deal with it."

"Go ahead," the second guy prodded, "as if anybody will care."

"Right, because we're strangers," Walker repeated.

"Absolutely."

Just then a voice filled his head. *Tell him McClintock would care.* Walker shuffled that around for a moment and then received a hard poke from inside. He glared, yet followed through with the suggestion. "I'm thinking McClintock would care," he murmured, and the response was electric.

The second guy turned nervously toward the first one. "Well, shit," he muttered. The two hired local thugs both looked slightly sick.

"So, will you talk now?" Walker asked, curious as shit now and wondering who this McClintock guy was, given their reaction to his name.

"Look. They just wanted to know what you were up to. Nobody here likes strangers in town."

"I don't believe you," Walker said.

"That's all I've got for you," the second guy replied in

exasperation. "We got a phone call, telling us it was worth a couple hundred bucks to find out what you were up to because they'd heard about strangers lurking in town."

"So, that's how you guys treat visitors, is it?" Calum asked curiously. "I saw a lot of tourists when we came into town, and two men like us will hardly cause all kinds of headaches for you, unless you deserve them."

"But we don't know that," the second man argued smoothly. "And obviously our bosses didn't know that."

"*Right,*" Walker quipped in disgust. "I've got a message for you and your bosses. We're here, and we'll do whatever we want to do, and nothing they can do will stop us. Now, with that out of the way, if we see you on our tails again, we'll haul you to jail. How's that?"

"You didn't haul us to jail now, so I highly doubt that threat held any water."

"Maybe not but McClintock will be informed."

At that, they both looked at each other nervously.

"I suggest you get lost," Calum stated, releasing the second man. "Remember to take that message back to your bosses."

"We also want the young man returned to us," Walker added, "and, if we find out you had anything to do with the kidnapping, believe me, this little meeting tonight will be the easiest of the things you'll face in the next ten years."

And, with that, both men took off and raced around the corner.

Walker looked over at Calum. "What the hell's going on?"

"I'm not sure," Calum admitted, then looked over at him. "Where did you get that name from?"

Walker snorted. "I would have said Terkel, but there was

an extra feminine push, like an impatient poke when I didn't fork over the name, so I'm pretty sure that was Ashley in my head. And what the hell is that about, when people can just turn up in your head and start talking? You know, for somebody who's very antisocial, Ashley sure got pushy in a hurry."

Calum looked at him and smirked. "She didn't pop into my brain," he said.

"Yeah, believe me. I noticed. However, the name *McClintock* did provoke a very interesting reaction from our tails."

"It sure did, but now I just want to know who this McClintock guy is," Calum admitted, "because it sounds as if he might be the power on this island and someone who would be good to have on our side."

Walker grimaced. "Doesn't mean it's a power that would be on our side though. It could just be a name that raises a lot of fear."

"Sure, which also means, chances are, he's not one of the good guys, and that's a whole different story."

"Exactly," Walker muttered, "and we don't really have very much to go on."

"So, are we going to the motel, or are we heading back to talk to our lady healer who gave us the name?" Just then Calum's phone rang. He pulled it from his pocket, looked at the screen, and smiled. "Hello, Ashley."

"You don't need to come back here," she stated, her tone clear and crisp. "McClintock is waiting for you." She quickly gave him an address. "You've got twenty minutes, so get your butts over there," and, with that, she ended the call. Calum looked over at Walker. "I don't know what her game is, but her methodology is certainly clear."

"Who is this McClintock?" Walker muttered.

"We're supposed to go find out, apparently," Calum replied, punching in the address she'd given him to his phone. The address came up as only a few blocks away. "It's nearby, so let's go take a look and see what this guy has to do with this mess," Calum suggested. "If nothing else, the fact that he got that kind of response from our tails makes me curious to meet him."

"You might be curious to meet him," Walker countered, "but that doesn't mean that we should be walking into this, trusting her."

"True, and that's a point I'm quite aware of," Calum muttered. "However, I'm not sure we have a whole lot of choice at this point."

"Yeah, but we also don't know, and I hate to say this, but we don't know that she didn't have something to do with that young man's disappearance." Somebody smacked him—psychically—on the side of the head. In his brain, he roared and smacked back almost instinctively. An odd silence came in his head, and then he muttered, "Enough of that," he snapped—out loud.

At Calum's frown, Walker glared at his partner. "She just smacked me … hard, so I smacked her back."

Calum was dumbfounded for a second, then his eyebrows shot up. "Wow, you guys have an interesting relationship already."

"It's not a relationship. *That* would be built on respect." There was an odd pulse in his jaw, then a laugh rippled through, and he sighed. "Now I think she's laughing at me."

"Yeah, it sounds like it," Calum added comfortably. "This is getting more and more fascinating by the second."

"Glad you're having fun," Walker muttered. "I can't say

that I am."

"I'm definitely having fun. This is mesmerizing. Okay, let's go." And, with that, they headed off to McClintock's address.

CHAPTER 3

ASHLEY PROBABLY SHOULDN'T have let them know that she could talk to them telepathically, but knowing that at least the one who worked for Terkel would have understood, she had assumed the other one would as well. Still, it seemed that she'd surprised Walker, and that was okay too. She hated it when people got so smug and complacent that they forgot that people were around who could do all kinds of things.

Still, she shouldn't have smacked him. That was uncalled for. The fact that he'd turned around and had smacked her right back was hilarious, yet also admirable. Not that she would ever condone anybody smacking a lady in real life, but she had certainly deserved it, and a smack energywise at that level wasn't like a physical assault. It was a nudge to *mind your own business*, like a boundaries reminder, which made her action even more unacceptable. She hadn't honored Walker's boundaries at all, so it made sense that he wouldn't honor hers.

Yet she had to admire somebody who could learn as quickly as he had, and, since she had tested it slightly already, it looked as if he had managed to shut the door between them. That was okay too. She could push it open if she had to, but she wouldn't want to push to that level if she didn't need to. What she needed was to call McClintock and to let him know these guys were coming. She quickly dialed the number that she knew by heart and smiled when he answered, his tone jolly.

"What can I do for you, sweetheart?"

She chuckled. "It's nice to know there's always a warm welcome when I call you."

"Hey, there would be a lot warmer welcome if you'd let me into your life," he teased, with his customary happy-go-lucky energy, "but you won't let me get in the door. Why is that?"

"No thank you," she said. "That is not a conversation we'll be having because we're simply not meant to be together."

"Ah, but you don't know until you try, and I know you've got all kinds of skills," he muttered. "Still, it's a little unnerving that you won't even give me a shot."

"Nope, I won't. Heads-up. Two men are coming to you right now. I gave them your name, and they used it when speaking to a couple men, who were following them."

"Interesting," he replied, his tone sharpening. "Why were they being followed?"

"I'm not sure," she muttered. "But I do know that your name creates all kinds of reactions, and, in this case, the two tails were particularly daunted at the thought of you finding out what they were up to."

"Oh, *great*. Were they my men?"

"I don't know. You'll have to ask. I don't have pictures and didn't even check to see if I knew them," she shared, "which is also kind of curious. I found myself more concerned about the other two. That in itself was interesting."

"So, what is this I hear about somebody going missing? Is that related?" he asked, his tone still brisk.

"I had an appointment scheduled for a young man who needed healing," she explained, her tone soft. "He didn't show up, and that was two days ago."

McClintock pondered that. "Any idea what happened?" he asked.

"No, but I can tell you that's what these men are here for. The young man is the brother of a friend of theirs," she shared, trying to be more direct, "so they're looking for him."

"That's understandable," he replied. "When a person goes missing, you would like to think that somebody would be looking for them."

"Exactly," she murmured. "I don't know who hired the two tails and what for, and there was no sign of foul play … up until the new guys were followed."

"So, they confronted these two locals?"

"They did, indeed, and the tails' story was that strangers in town weren't welcome, but eventually they admitted to being paid to find out what the two guys were up to."

"Curiouser and curiouser," McClintock said, with no inflection.

"Exactly, which is why I sent the new guys to you."

"Sounds like maybe they're here now," he added, "I'm just walking to my front door. Well, look at that. A vehicle is pulling up and parking outside my front door."

"Good. If you can help them out somehow, I would appreciate it."

"What's this young man to you?"

"Somebody who came to me for help," she stated, her tone calm and not giving anything else away. "You know how I feel about the people who come to me."

"Right, if they come to you, then they deserve help."

"Not even *deserve* help so much, but they get it because a lot of people never quite make it to this point."

"I still have to figure that one out someday," he muttered. "I don't even understand how you do what you do."

"It doesn't matter whether you do or not. And I don't recall ever asking how you do what you do either," she pointed out, a note of humor in her tone.

"True, and I get that. I guess both of our government days were long ago."

"Yes, and, by the way, one of these men is on Terkel's team."

"Terkel," he repeated, his tone darkening.

"Yes, but Terkel no longer works for the government." When silence came, she smiled at that. "Yes, I'm serious. Terk's gone private, after his own government tried to completely take out his whole team. I guess they all survived the attack, and my understanding is he's gone private."

"Damn, his government turned on him?"

"Yeah, the *government*. So, it's not common knowledge, but Terk is independent, and his entire team is with him."

"Ha, and is he still doing that woo-woo stuff?"

"Yeah, he's still doing that woo-woo stuff. He's doing it because he can't *not* do it," she stated. "It's who he is, and we both know it's who he'll always be."

"He was always one scary dude," McClintock muttered. "Somehow he knew things that nobody should have known."

"When you use people like that to bury the bodies, they have a tendency to remember where they're buried."

McClintock laughed at that. "Don't we all," he muttered. "Don't we all." And, with that, he ended the call.

Calum GOT OUT of the car and pointed up at the house. "Interesting that he's standing there in the doorway, talking to somebody on the phone."

"What do you want to bet it's Ashley?" Walker suggested.

Calum looked at him sharply. "And you know that how?"

"I don't know it at all. It's just my best guess. She sent us to him, which means she knows him, which means she's probably giving him notice."

"Yeah, but is it a friendly notice or not? I don't know about you, but my vision of this trip completely changed, once we found out we were being followed."

"It wouldn't be shocking if we were being followed right now," Walker declared. "Still, it may be a good thing because it backs up what we said we would do, which is to talk to McClintock. … Who is this McClintock anyway?" he muttered.

Calum nodded. "Yeah, I was wondering that myself. I'm not sure we'll ever find out, and he doesn't exactly look friendly."

"No, he sure doesn't." Walker studied the man in front of them, all six foot four and an easy 260 pounds of him. "He also looks like he's seen a little too much."

Calum replied, "You can't blame a man for seeking a peaceful lifestyle now."

"If that's what this is," Walker muttered. He walked up and greeted the man. "Hello, Ashley sent us over here to see you."

At that, McClintock stepped back and nodded. "Welcome. I understand you threw my name around today."

"At her suggestion," Walker said, with a wince, "I wouldn't even have known the name otherwise."

"That's a good thing," McClintock noted. "After you leave here, you might want to forget you ever heard it."

"That's not a problem. I can promise you that."

McClintock smiled. "Glad to see you learn fast."

"Oh, I do, but the question I have is, why were we followed in the first place?"

"Are you thinking I had something to do with it?" McClintock asked.

"I have no idea if you did or didn't," Walker admitted. "If you did, then I guess these guys are in trouble for getting caught. However, I presume that, if you were hiring someone to do such a task, they would have done a hell of a lot better job of it."

He snorted at that. "Yeah, you could say so. I really don't like to hire fools."

"None of us do," Walker agreed, with a nod.

"That doesn't mean that we're so lucky as to have staff or contractors available who can do a damn job," McClintock clarified.

"These two were stupid, … and they're afraid of you."

At that, McClintock smiled. "I'm not against having anybody I hire be afraid of me, particularly if they screw up."

At that, both of the men just studied him carefully and didn't say anything more.

McClintock eyed them and in a measured tone asked, "You're here for the young man then?"

"We are. Do you know anything about him?"

He shook his head. "I don't, but I just heard from Ashley that this young man has gone missing, and apparently nobody knows where he is."

"That's what we've heard and what we're trying to get to the bottom of. He's apparently quite ill, even to the point that he has possibly curled up and died along the road somewhere. However, after picking up a tail as soon as we got here, I don't think it's likely."

McClintock nodded. "Another reason for those two to get their asses kicked. They've conceivably completely changed the game, if somebody is involved in foul play."

"They did, indeed," Calum stated, staring at McClintock, standing in front of them. "Though I guess I should say that they aren't the kind I would ever hire anyway."

"Why is that?" McClintock asked.

"The one is a drinker, and the second one seemed he didn't give a crap and hated his partner."

"Ah, sounds to me that we're talking about the Yagermite brothers." McClintock nodded. "They generally do jobs for anybody who's got a couple bucks to give them to keep them in booze. One can't stand the other because he's an alcoholic, yet he drinks just as much."

Calum nodded. "Could be the Yagermites. I really don't know who they were, and I didn't particularly care to hang around with them long enough to figure it out."

"You don't like to know who your enemies are?"

"Those lackeys aren't our enemies," Walker declared. "Whoever hired them? Now that's a different story." The two men measured McClintock.

"I didn't hire them." McClintock smiled. "I can assure you of that. They're useless, but I also haven't heard much about this missing person, so I will put out some feelers. I'll let Ashley know if anybody comes up with anything."

"That would be helpful," Calum replied, with a nod. "Sorry for disturbing your evening." And, with that, he walked back to their vehicle.

In the meantime, Walker studied the man in front of him. "I presume she's not in any danger?"

At that, McClintock looked at him with half a smile. "No, she's not in any danger, but I'll let her know you care."

"Do that," he agreed, "not that she won't already know I'm asking anyway."

At that, McClintock burst out laughing. "She's a dandy, that one, all right. No sense trying to pull anything over on her."

"And yet she lost an appointment anyway," he stated harshly. "It makes me wonder whether the young man was the target, or she was."

At that, McClintock's face narrowed in concentration. "Now that's a thought—not one I particularly like."

"I don't like it either. I get that she wants to live a private life, but it could be possible that somebody's trying to force her out of that early retirement."

McClintock stared at Walker intently, his gaze giving no quarter, yet searching to see what Walker was about. When McClintock settled back, he gave a clipped nod, acknowledging the idea. "I'll keep that in mind."

At that, Walker headed back to the car.

Calum now walked beside him, not speaking until they got into the car. "You want to explain that one to me?" Calum asked.

"That would be a little hard," Walker admitted, "but definitely something is going on here between the two of them."

"You think they're together? Like in a relationship?"

"No, I don't think so, but he's very protective of her. From where I am at, that's both good and bad because I'm not sure whom is after who in this scenario."

"You could have told me that you thought somebody was after her," Calum said, offended.

"It only occurred to me while I was standing there looking at McClintock, realizing that he is someone who would look after Ashley—in case this gets ugly. I wanted to ensure he had a heads-up that such a thing was possible."

"Good enough," Calum acknowledged. "Now, if it's okay with you, I suggest we head back to the motel, grab some sleep while we can, then start again early in the morning."

"I'm all for that." Walker then winced, his head dropping forward, as yet another vision slammed into him. When he could finally breathe, he gingerly raised his head.

Calum watched him in concern, though when he spoke, his tone was calm. "You want to tell me what that was all about?" Calum asked.

"As soon as I catch my breath," Walker gasped, as he shifted uneasily in the seat.

"How far away is that precog session?"

"I don't know," he gasped again, still caught up in the last vestiges of it.

"You have no control over it, do you?"

"No, most of us don't," he muttered in disgust. "If I did have any control, believe me, I would have stopped it a long time ago."

"You don't like it?"

"No, not only that, when you have no control over something like this, you also can't change the outcome."

"That's not true," Calum denied, "at least according to

Terkel. When you have that knowledge, you should do something about it. Not always but sometimes."

"I sure as hell hope so," Walker replied, "because that vision showed Ashley getting shot."

At that, Calum pulled off to the side of the road to gaze at him carefully. "You got any time frame?"

"No," he muttered. "And telling her won't make a damn bit of difference because she just won't listen."

"What do you want to do?"

"I don't know what I want to do because I don't know what I'm supposed to do. What do you do with that information?"

Calum slowly started the vehicle and headed back to the motel. "If you think that's happening tonight—"

"I can't tell you that," Walker barked. "All I can tell you is that, when we get back to the motel, I'll contact her and give her a word of warning. She'll ignore me anyway, so the only thing I can do for now is potentially warn McClintock."

"You think he'll listen?"

"No, I don't think he'll listen necessarily, but an extra set of eyes won't hurt at this point."

"I agree with you there," Calum muttered. "Damn."

They pulled into the small motel parking lot, and Walker got out slowly, stretching his legs and trying to kick the kinks out. He felt exhausted. Every time he took a trip into a precognition, the aftereffects could be pretty rough. This one had come hard and fast and had more or less just slammed into him without any warning. That was fine and dandy, except for coming back out again.

If anybody out here wanted to attack him, now would be a hell of a time to do it because Walker was still caught up in that energy. Following Calum toward the back of the motel, as they walked, he grabbed Calum's arm and pulled.

Calum looked at him, on alert.

"Our room," Walker whispered, wincing as yet more energy slammed into his brain. "Christ, I'm not sure why it's so damn strong over here."

"It doesn't matter. Stay here. Recover. I'll go up."

"No," he muttered. "I'm coming."

"What good will that do?"

"I don't know, but I feel that I need to come."

And, with that, Calum wouldn't argue, so they both raced to their room. When they got there, they positioned themselves on either side of the door. On the count of three, they burst into the room, only to hear scurrying feet going out the window. Calum jumped toward the window and headed out after the intruder, while Walker looked around to see what the intruder had been after.

A little bit of their stuff had been moved around, but that was it, and all of it had been searched. Their bags were opened and dumped on the beds, their clothing tossed. Calum and Walker had had their laptops with them, so this was just their personal gear.

When Calum came back inside, his face was grim. "He had a driver waiting."

"That's probably how the intruder knew we were here. He got a heads-up from the driver."

"It's quite possible," Calum agreed, as he looked around. "Any idea what they were after?"

"They opened our bags, but nothing here for them to grab." Walker frowned at Calum. "The stakes just went up."

"In a big way."

Walker quickly snatched his phone and started dialing.

"Who are you calling?"

"Ashley," he muttered. "You might want to bring Terkel up to speed." When Ashley answered the phone, her tone was slow, as if coming out of the deep meditation of a healing state. "Heads up, our place was searched, and I had a precog vision about you being attacked. Shot actually, so this is about the only warning I can give you. Watch your ass."

She gasped. "What?"

"Yeah, you heard me. We just got back from meeting McClintock and found an intruder in our room. The place had been searched, our belongings dumped," he described, looking around at the mess. "We went out after him, but he had a vehicle to jump into. No idea if it was the same men following us or not."

"Wow, I don't know what the heck's going on or why anybody is doing this. We've had no problems for a very long time."

"But that doesn't mean that no problems will ever come," Walker argued. "So you need to tell me what the hell the last problem was."

"Why?" she asked, her tone hard. "It doesn't apply to anything happening now."

"Are you sure about that? Because I mentioned to McClintock one possibility I'm sure you won't like. He didn't like it much either. What are the chances that this kidnapping has nothing to do with Frank and everything to do with you?"

CHAPTER 4

ASHLEY SAGGED INTO the big easy chair in front of the window and stared aimlessly at the gorgeous view in front of her—a view that had always brought out the joy, quiet, comfort, that sense of being home. She was counting on it right now because the last thing she wanted was to feel that fear, stress, and trauma of the panic that had overtaken her for so long.

She'd worked for the government under duress, far longer than she should have, ending up with PTSD symptoms for years. This place was her solace. Until somebody had found her here some years back. It was a problem she thought she had dealt with, and yet now it was coming back for her.

No, her brain screamed, *that's not true. You don't know that. You're afraid that's what's happening, but you don't know that to be true. You're functioning on fear, and you need to shift that.* That warning was correct; she did need to shift her earlier thoughts, but that was not exactly an easy thing to do. Shifting them meant acknowledging them and sharing them, which she was not interested in doing at all. However, she also knew that Walker and Calum wouldn't let this go, and, if Frank's disappearance had something to do with what had initially gone so wrong in her world five years ago, then maybe facing this was something she had to do.

When her phone rang again, she stared down at it, her expression a grimace. She knew no way Walker would let it go, not when he was after something. She answered it, her tone heavy.

"I'm not trying to hassle you," he began, his tone calm, quiet, almost soothing, "but considering the precog vision I had of you being shot, I'm not happy leaving this as is."

She gave a startled laugh. "What do you expect me to say to that? You don't even know who I am or anything about me."

"I do know a lot about you," he declared, his tone never wavering. "I know that you're somebody who functions from a specific point of energy. I know that you're somebody who cares and somebody who's tried hard to isolate herself away from the hurt that seems to be never-ending, threatening to destroy that precious peace of mind in your soul."

She sucked in her breath at that.

Walker continued. "I know this is becoming a little too close for comfort, but hiding away won't help us find this young man."

She winced at that. "I'm not stopping you from finding him, but I don't see how any of this is relevant."

"What I have found in life is, when we come to the crux of the matter, it doesn't matter what is relevant to us. It's all about what is relevant to whoever is behind this. That is what's important. I get that you don't want to open up that can of worms in your past. I do. I am not saying you have to face whatever it is that happened back then, but, for the sake of this young man who is missing and who needs your help, I'm hoping you will. I understand that, for you, you've always held on to the *if he needed me, he would be here* philosophy, but that's assuming that nothing in your world was stopping him from getting to you. Right now, I suspect something very much like that is happening, and that somebody is doing their best to either keep Frank from reaching you or to keep you from doing what it is that you do."

He was almost right to say that, and she understood it completely.

"The sooner you take a closer look at that, the sooner we can all work together to move this forward. I know you don't like the intrusion on your best shot at a peaceful existence, and I'm sorry for that, but something will happen whether you like it or not, and you've got to understand that too."

She hated the caring inflection in his tone, though it was completely wrapped up in a certain level of hardness, as if to will her to do what he wanted her to do. But that caring would be her undoing, and she didn't even think he realized it was there. "I'll think about it," she replied abruptly.

"You'll have to think fast." Then he disconnected.

She knew he was right because, damn it, this young man had come to her, and everything was blowing up in his face. The idea that he might not make it because of some other problem—*her* problem—was sure to devastate her.

Ashley sighed. She worked on the basis of *healing*, not on the basis of *hurting*. Yet so much of the world around her didn't care about that. They only wanted to hurt and to resolve whatever bothered them. They wanted what they wanted, and it didn't matter who got hurt in the process. Unfortunately, it started to feel very much like that was what was going on.

Ashley sat here, frozen, for a long time, then slowly picked up the phone and called McClintock. "Do you have any idea who the men were who followed them?" she asked.

"I have an idea, but I haven't confirmed it. Why?"

"Because the new guys are afraid that it may have something to do with me, and I'm sure that you know how that'll make me feel."

"But it's still not your fault. We're right back to that same old garbage from our work. Just because assholes are out in the world and will do anything to hurt people, and they choose to hurt people we're involved with, all that doesn't mean that we are at fault or are responsible."

"No, maybe not," she conceded, "but I didn't understand the logic then, and I can't really work with it now either."

He groaned. "Fine, no point talking to you about it back then, and I know that won't change. What is it you want to do right now?"

"I'm not sure," she whispered. "I just want this to go away. I want that young man back here, where I can work to help him, and I don't want the past to raise its ugly head again."

Then came a long silence. "I don't think the past will raise its head," McClintock shared, his tone almost too detached.

Then she whispered, "Are you sure?"

"I'm very sure," he said briskly. "You know that I took care of him a long time ago."

His wording made her wince. "The way you said that is enough to make me break out in hives," she joked.

"You didn't want to know anything about it, so I didn't tell you."

"Right, until we get to that part where I'm still guilty by omission."

"You're not guilty of anything," he said in exasperation.

"Now, go to bed and get some sleep. The past won't raise its ugly head." And, with that, he ended the call.

She stared down at the phone, terrified of what might be coming, knowing it would completely destroy any progress she had made in the last five years. She had tried so hard, had worked so diligently to put all that into perspective. She had buried it deep, so she could work on the healing that was really her forte. Yet how did one heal anyone when all that shit was going on around you? Particularly if healing came up against what she was sadly afraid had been murder.

WALKER STARED DOWN at the phone and looked over at Calum. "She's hiding something."

Calum nodded. "Everybody does."

"I know everybody does, but in this case it'll affect our ability to find Frank."

"That could be," Calum admitted, looking over at him. "You got any idea how to make her give it up?"

He laughed. "I think her years in the government, in whatever capacity she worked, has more or less ruined her for any kind of cooperation."

"I don't think you can force her either," Calum added, studying him carefully. "I'm not saying she's immune to it, but I think she's been tortured in many ways for a long time. She's healing now, and she's come a long way to get out of whatever nightmare she was in, but she's not there yet."

Walker sighed. "I get it, and she's definitely not there yet."

"She's very protective of her own space, but what do we do about Kim's brother? Then, there is your ... vision, precog or whatever."

"These precogs just won't leave me alone."

Calum's gaze sharpened. "Did you get another one?"

"No, not a complete one. It was just … I don't even know what it is," he muttered. "It's this weird sense."

"Maybe you could elaborate a little bit," Calum murmured. "Remember? This is what we do."

"I know. Are you getting anything?"

"No, I'm sure not," Calum admitted, "but I'm very aware that this is your ball game."

"What does that mean?" Walker asked.

"It means that I'm here as a ground for you," Calum stated bluntly. "Sure, there might be some things that I can do if we get into trouble, but this is very much your deal. I'm here to support Kim and to help find her brother in any way possible, even if that means letting her know the worst happened. That would be very unfortunate, but Frank is very sick, so there may not be anything we can do, since we are not healers. But not doing something because there's nothing we can do is a very different story from other people having done something because they could."

"Is that what you think has happened?"

"I'm not sure," Calum admitted in frustration. "The fact that I can't tell you anything makes me even angrier."

"Anger is definitely not helpful." Walker turned and glared at Calum, who just shrugged.

"You and I both know that."

"Yeah, I know that. Remember that part about it's not helping?"

Calum flashed him a grin. "Yeah, remember that part about I'm just here to help?"

"Yeah, I hear you, but so far the help isn't helping."

Calum burst out laughing at that. "So, go back to the beginning. Figure out what the next step is, and we'll go from there."

"How am I supposed to know what the next step is?"

"Seems we need to do a history on Ashley, and maybe on this McClintock, who appears to be so close to her. Maybe that would tell us where the problem is."

"I can already tell you some stuff. She worked for the government, and everybody has done a hell of a job burying that fact, and she's trying to move on."

"Yet she can't because …?"

"Because of her history, because of something in the past. She's done whatever she needed to do in order to open up for healing, but it's possible that other people around her haven't done something. As long as she can clear herself, then potentially she can continue to heal."

"According to what Terkel told me, she's an incredibly strong healer."

"And the world needs those, but Terkel also mentioned that a lot of people in this world can't heal, even though they should be able to, simply because of the negative energy in their own space. If she is healing, chances are, she's done an awful lot to clear out any negativity."

"What are you saying then?" Calum asked Walker.

"I don't want to send her backward, to push her back there by bringing it all up again," he said. "I'm just not sure what our options are."

"Exactly. We'll push some buttons because people are hiding crap again. As we know, it's fairly common, but it's not helpful."

"It's never helpful," Walker snapped. "Damn it, I don't know why I'm so affected by this." He turned and glared at

Calum.

Calum just stared back at him. "What are you glaring at me for?"

"Because you're laughing at me," he accused.

"No, I'm not laughing at you, but it's definitely interesting to see you like this."

"Why?"

"Because you know what's wrong, but you won't listen to it."

He stiffened. "So now you're the psychic?"

"Of course I'm psychic," Calum declared, with a wave of his hand, "but that doesn't mean that I can produce answers on demand any more than you can. I just know that whatever is going on between you two is personal, and that's the doorway you don't want to open."

He stiffened. "Nothing is between us."

"Energy is arcing between you, and that means something is there. Whether it's of this lifetime or another," Calum explained, his tone calm and flat. "It's up to you guys to decide if you'll do anything to pursue it. I can see from her perspective that you're not somebody she wants to be with because you deal with this stuff, and I think her whole world has been overly impacted by that."

He stared at Calum, then sank onto the side of his bed. "Maybe," he admitted, his tone distant. "But having a relationship with somebody involved in a case isn't exactly a pathway I want to pursue. And just because I can see energy between us doesn't mean that energy should be picked up, warmed up, and a connection built."

"No, absolutely not, but I would say it definitely is something you could do in order to get answers."

Walker stiffened.

"No, I'm not talking about seducing her to get answers or anything like that, but she's a fool and not the healer that I believe her to be if she isn't picking up on that same energy. While you're here, and you have a chance to find out who this Ashley person is, and what's important to her, I think you would be making a mistake not to pursue that avenue and see just what there is between you."

"Coming from a man who is now very happily married?" Walker asked, staring at Calum. "You know yourself that if somebody would have told you that years ago, you would have told them to *eff off.*"

"I probably would have," he agreed, with a smile. "Absolutely I would have because I believed with all my heart that it was too dangerous to have a partner. It was too dangerous to bring someone I loved into this field because our enemies would go after them."

At that, Walker began to understand that a story was behind that. "Did it happen?"

"Absolutely," Calum confirmed. "And that was a reminder that bad shit happens anyway. So it's important to enjoy the days that you have together and to do everything you can to keep your family and your loved ones safe. And often having them safe means keeping them close. You're a long way from being close to Ashley, but there is that thread of potential. Do you want to pursue that thread, or do you want to walk away and never know what it's like to have what I have?" As Calum spoke, he stared at Walker face-to-face. "I've got to tell you, that would be a hell of a shame."

CHAPTER 5

ASHLEY WANTED TO believe that sleep would come at some point tonight, but the evidence was proving otherwise. As she shifted uneasily once again, she got up and went into the living room to stare out of her window, searching for that sense of calm, that sense of complacency, or at least ease, but it wasn't coming.

Something stirred on the horizon, something ugly, and, having seen it time and time again, Ashley was more than a little worried as to where this would end up. She waited until 6:00 a.m. before contacting McClintock. When he answered, she knew that he'd been up for hours already.

"So, you still aren't at peace?" he asked.

"No," she murmured. "It's worse. The feeling is just plain wrong."

He sighed. "I haven't been able to get any sleep myself, so I can't say I'm surprised."

She sighed. "Is there anything I can do?"

"You should be the one to tell me that," he replied, with a note of humor. "I don't have anything to offer."

"And that is a little dubious," she murmured, "because, if anybody should have something to offer, it should be you, since you always have your finger on the pulse of what's going on."

"I thought I did," he said, his tone calm, "but I'm not

sure what's happening right now. I know that's not what you want to hear, but I don't know what else to say."

"It's really just a matter of how we're planning to handle whatever is coming at us."

He hesitated and then asked, "And you're sure of it, right?"

"Very sure," she murmured. "I don't know what it is. I just know it's already on the way, … and it's coming for me."

"Time frame?" he asked, his tone that of somebody who had worked with her for a long time. It was brisk, lethal, and clearly meant business.

"Less than two days," she replied. "I'm sitting in front of my window, trying to find that calm, that center, for whatever is happening."

"When you get more information, let me know," he stated. "In the meantime, I guess I have some information to look up. I'll let you know what I come up with." With that, he was gone.

She remained there, staring out into the beautiful early morning light. A beauty she knew was deceptive this time. Something very ugly was out there and heading toward her at a speed that left her gasping. That it was quite likely part of her history was disturbing, since she'd gone to a lot of effort in order to ensure none of that ever came back to her. That much was grace, that she had been free and clear of this for five years, but now something was catching up. Being free and clear was important, a salvation. Knowing there would be life after all this nightmare would give her some hope, but, so far, it didn't look very promising.

Just when she thought she was calming down and life could get a little easier, her phone rang. She looked down at the number, hating the fact that she didn't even need to see her phone screen to know it was Walker. She hesitated, then up popped a familiar voice in her head.

Really no point in not answering.

She groaned. "*Great*, thanks, Terkel."

You're welcome. You and I both know that, when certain things are coming toward us, they can't be stopped.

She answered the phone and snapped, "What?"

Startled, Walker regrouped. "Good morning."

"Yeah, good morning to you too," she murmured. "I'm still not any happier to hear your voice than I was last night. Just putting that out there."

"I'm sorry for that, but it really doesn't matter. A life is at stake."

"Unless that life is already lost," she added, trying hard to stay calm at the thought.

"It is not lost," he murmured, "but it could be, if we don't get help."

"What help is it you want from me? I was here, ready and available. I'm not sure I have anything more to give."

He hesitated at that, then whispered, "Are you sure about that?"

She hated that somebody might understand what she'd gone through and what she was going through now. "What is it you want from me?"

"Anything you have to give," he murmured, his tone warm and caring. "I didn't expect this connection between us, you know? I wasn't looking for it, but, if this is what's ahead of me, I'm not walking away."

She gave a startled laugh. "You don't even know what *this* is. You don't know anything about me," she uttered, "and I'm not in any way ready to discuss something like that.

If you want something in regard to this young man, and it's something I can give, then I will possibly help. I say *possibly* only because I don't know what you're asking of me." She added with finality, "Honestly, I'm not sure I have much actual help to give."

"I've heard that a time or two," he murmured. "Have you talked to McClintock this morning?"

"I have," she replied, then waited.

Walker gave a half laugh. "Did he have any insights? Anything that could help?"

"No, at least nothing that he told me. Maybe you should talk to him yourself."

"I will. I'm working on it."

"Right, maybe you should work a little faster."

"No need to be nasty. We are trying over here."

"Of course you are, but it feels as if you expect me to have answers."

"Not at all," he corrected, startled. "It would be nice if you had something to offer, but, if you don't, you don't. I just know that it involves you, and I feel that you haven't been completely honest with us. But, if you aren't with us, you're against us, and that'll be a problem."

His logic left her gasping. "Do you think it's quite so easy?" she asked.

"No, I don't think it's easy at all, but I do think it's doable, and fundamental things remain important. This young man has a chance at life, and he has family who loves him—a family who wasn't even aware that he was making this journey because he believes so strongly in it but knew that people around him wouldn't be of the same mind."

"Of course most people aren't. So, imagine what it's like to be a healer."

"I've been told about Cara and Clary, who work with Terkel. They are of the same opinion and have worked in the shadows, just as much as you have, knowing that you can't really pop up and advertise what you do and that there is never enough of you to go around in a world that's broken. But you can heal some things, for some people, some of the time, and, if there's something you can do right now, we need you to do it."

Long after she ended the call with him, Walker's words still reverberated through her mind. She wasn't even sure she could do anything at this point. She didn't have anything, no direction to go, no sign of what to do. It was one thing if a person stood in front of you who needed healing, and it was a clear-cut case of cancer, with lymphomas or whatever was troubling that poor soul. But to have something nebulous, like a missing person, was not in her wheelhouse.

Just then Terkel's voice popped into her head. *Can you scan Frank from a distance?*

She jolted at the idea. "I might be able to," she said cautiously. "Why?"

It might help us to understand whether he's alive or dead, do we have a chance to save him, or is it likely already too late, he murmured. *Any information at this point is something we can use.*

"Your people can't do it?" she asked cautiously.

You are right there in close proximity. Plus, you already have a connection with him. I don't know that I want to bring any other people into this, but, if I have to, I will.

She snorted. "In other words, if I don't do it, you'll go over my head and do it anyway."

We're not working for the government anymore, he reminded her. *This is the free world, where it's all about helping people because we can. Not because we must follow orders or do what we're told. I get that you're still dealing with an awful lot of aftershocks from that and that you probably haven't had an easy time moving away from all that headache, but, right now, this isn't about what other people are telling us to do. This is about us doing what's right for that young man.*

"Is he a friend of yours too?"

No, I don't know him. He's the brother of a friend, and, yes, these are good people. They fight the good fight all over the world every day, and, if there's anything we can do for this young man, I would like to do it. I would at least like to tell his sister that we've done everything we can. I could bring in more boots on the ground, but that will take time.

"Right, and of course you would do that," she murmured.

Look. You tried to hide, and, for a while, you even managed to stay hidden, but you can't hide any longer. This world is here in front of us, and, whether we like it or not, the world has found you, and it won't let go just because you want it to. I know that it doesn't seem fair, but you and I both know it never matters when it comes to fair. And, with that, he disappeared.

Ashley sat here for a long moment, feeling different parts of her at war with each other. She wanted to help, but she'd never really done anything like this before. That didn't mean it wasn't possible. In fact, she was pretty-darn sure that not only was it possible but maybe quite doable. From what Terk had said, it sounded like he had people who could do something similar, but that maybe it was easier if in close proximity to the subject needing healing.

Professionally she was curious about that aspect, yet she knew that wasn't the right reason to go into something like this, but how did one not find a certain level of curiosity as to what one could really do? However, she'd tamped down her abilities for the longest time because, as soon as her bosses found out she could do anything, she'd been forced into developing it at a rate much bigger and faster than was comfortable or even safe. It made her never want to experiment or to broaden her skills, staying hidden, frozen in time, rather than developing gifts that other people could exploit.

Yet Terkel was right. They were in a whole new world now.

She just hadn't stepped into it.

She'd stayed hidden out in the ethers, doing her thing, without worrying about other people, because she'd been able to fly under the radar. That's why she hadn't advertised, why she hadn't let anybody know, just in case the government ever found her again.

At that, she stiffened, then quickly sent McClintock a text message, asking if there was any chance the government was doing this.

He phoned her right away. "Do you really think that's an issue?"

"I don't know. It just came to my mind over something that Terkel has asked me to do."

"Terkel," he repeated, with wonder. "That man is a force to be reckoned with."

"He is, and I'll attempt to do something, but it brought to mind the fact that, if the government is involved, … I don't want them finding me."

"They can't find you now," he stated easily.

"You keep saying that, but I no longer have the same confidence."

"Ah, you wound me," he said instantly. "I've never let you down before, have I?"

"No," she replied, "you haven't. But, if this is something they are behind, it would mean that they've already found me."

"They found you a long time ago. I just didn't bother to tell you."

She gasped. "What do you mean?"

"We had a talk, and I let them know just how long it would be before I allowed them into your life again," he shared. "You were beyond traumatized and still trying to hide from them, so they decided it was much better to back off, than to sit there and bring on an all-out war."

"You seriously convinced them to leave?" she asked in shock.

"I did, and I think they've held to it."

She pondered that. "So, you don't think it has anything to do with them?"

"I don't," he declared, "but I'm not so sure that we don't have somebody who's gone rogue."

She winced at that. "The government was good at that too."

"Doing what?" he asked curiously.

"Sending their people rogue, when they couldn't do what they wanted to do. Yet there was always that expectation that we were supposed to do more. So many people had ideas that they could run and carry this off, but they needed to do it without the confines of the government overlords."

"Exactly. So there is always that chance."

"Right. I'll try and see if I can do what Terkel's asked of me, and, no, I won't tell you what it is because it won't make any sense anyway. But, if you hear any rumors from this point on, about the government or anything out there, please let me know."

With that, she disconnected, settled into place, and slowly reached out to the young man who had contacted her earlier.

CALUM LOOKED OVER at Walker. "We need to get some food, while everybody else is checking up on Ashley's background, her history, even McClintock's info, and whatever else they can get their hands on. Terkel found an awful lot of stuff that's been redacted, government databases wiped because of her involvement, but he's got everybody trying to get as much as they can in the meantime. So, meanwhile, I need food." He rubbed his stomach, which was already growling.

Walker added, "We also don't know what the day will bring, so it's time to tank up while we can."

At that, Calum nodded, and the two of them walked to the door.

"Still feels odd," Walker muttered.

They exited their motel room and headed up the street. Calum gave Walker time and space, as he obviously continued to ponder what was going on. "You're not getting anything?"

Walker shook his head. "Nothing specific, no. Just lots of the same again."

"Right, so no answers, but not anything obviously wrong."

"No," he replied cautiously, "but definitely an odd feeling."

"Something on the ethers is moving," Calum noted. "I can feel that."

"You feel that?" Walker asked.

Calum nodded. "I can feel it. I'm just not sure what I'm feeling."

"Right."

"That's the weird thing about this. Something is stirring out there."

Walker asked Calum, "Have you guys ever come up against anybody else who has skills like us but are working on the wrong side of life?"

Calum nodded. "We have, but they are in the minority, which is a good thing. You would like to think that what we have is an advantage in that case, but it's more that we're up against somebody who already has an advantage, then things get pretty ugly."

"I can imagine," he murmured. "Is that what you're sensing? Is it somebody else out there with energy?"

"I'm not sure what I'm sensing," Calum admitted. "Honestly, it just feels off."

"*Off* is one thing. *Wrong* is another way to phrase it, but none of it will do us any good until we get some real answers."

Calum laughed.

"Maybe we're picking up on something that Ashley's doing right now. I don't know what she's up to, but definitely some weirdness is going on. I don't really know how to explain it. It's just plain weird."

"*Weird* works," Calum noted cheerfully. They walked into the little café and ordered the special listed on the board. As soon as they sat down, he smiled at the waitress, who didn't look like she spoke much English, but she came back with a coffeepot in her hand, and they nodded, silently saying *Yes, please.* Then she left them.

Over coffee, Calum asked, "So, what are we supposed to do now?"

"Find the missing young man," Walker stated. "And, for that, we track his whereabouts. He almost checked in at our motel, but then he left with some unidentified person. So now we have to figure out where he went from there."

Calum nodded. "Terkel has checked, and no cameras are here. This is a small town, without much in the way of crime, so they don't have many people at the sheriff's office either. Therefore, we can't expect much help along that line."

"That's not helpful," Walker muttered.

"It never is," Calum agreed, "but we've seen it time and time again, so I can't say I'm particularly surprised."

Walker didn't say anything to that.

When their large breakfast arrived, they dug into the substantial platefuls of food. By the time they were halfway done, they were still pondering their next step.

Walker suggested, "Tracking where Frank's been would be very helpful, but, so far, nobody has any idea. What about checking with some of the businesses around here?"

"It's about the only move we have. We'll need to walk around with his photo, looking for anybody who has seen him. We'll be up against the same factors as before. We are strangers, and so is he, so potentially nobody'll care."

"I'm not so worried about that. I think there's a good chance someone will care. Not everybody is an asshole," Walker muttered. "It just seems like it sometimes."

At that, Calum laughed. "You're right. Not everybody is. Hopefully we'll find somebody who's seen Frank and who will give us a place to start. So, that's settled. As soon as breakfast is over, that's what we'll do. Unless you have something else that needs to be done instead."

Walker shrugged. "Not that I know of."

Calum just nodded and didn't say anything.

"Unless you're trying to tell me something," Walker added.

"I'm not trying to tell you anything," Calum replied, with a laugh, "but it's on you to speak up if there's something you need to do."

"Yeah, well, that would imply that I had more energy readings happening around my world right now that I could use, but all I'm getting is silence. No precog activity, no nothing. So, it's back to good old-fashioned stomping through town, asking questions."

"I'm good with that too." Calum smirked. "Oftentimes that is still the very best way we have to find answers."

"Yeah, but it's slow, and it's tedious, and a lot of people don't want to talk to us," Walker complained.

After breakfast they headed outside and started walking up the street. "It would help if we had better photos."

"I know, but what we have is the latest ones from Kim. They may not be great, but I'm sure he's still quite recognizable."

"Except that he's quite sick now."

They went from store to store, asking if anybody had seen the young man. Every time it was a no, a no, and another no. By the time they had finished asking all the employees and customers of the shops on the main streets, they shared a look.

Walker finally voiced it. "That's interesting."

"It makes me suspicious," Calum stated. "How is it that nobody knows anything? It's not as if this is a huge place."

"Do you think they've been threatened into silence or

something?"

"Not necessarily. It's more that they're willing to be silent, or something else is going on here that we know nothing about."

"And that would be what?"

Calum shrugged. "Your guess is as good as mine."

"Which isn't helpful, since I'm fresh out of guesses."

CHAPTER 6

THERE. ASHLEY HAD done what she could do, at least for the moment. Moving slowly, as if she'd aged one hundred years, she made her way into her simple bedroom, but, rather than just crash, she sat down on the nearest chair, not able to make it to her bed. Every movement was so hard, as if her bones were made of glass, because that's how she felt right now—fragile—as if everything around her was coalescing into this huge bubble, but a bubble heading toward a complete explosion, when whatever was going on caught up with her.

She just didn't know what it was or why … or in what way it would all implode. She had had nothing to do with anybody for the last five years, staying to herself, living a quiet and simple life, healing those who came to her. Ashley had ignored everybody else—or had tried to. She'd stayed close to McClintock, mostly because they had a work history already, before she'd gone into hiding, and he understood the type of work they had done. He had been all for her going to ground and had been one of the few people she kept her lifeline attached to, even when she felt as if there was no point in any of it anymore.

Now she needed him yet again, but in a way she hadn't expected. But to keep calling on him, to keep asking him for favors, just put her in a position she didn't want to be in. She knew he would laugh and would tell her to stop worrying about it, but she hated to be indebted to anybody. Particularly to somebody like him, who had power at his fingertips and utilized it willy-nilly as he needed to. She didn't want to owe him anything. That put her in an even worse position right now because she didn't know what to do with the weird feelings running through her.

After a rest, she finally made it to her bed.

When her phone rang, she ignored it, pulling the pillow over her head and crashing deeper and deeper, until she found the peace in the souls of a world without physical form, where she could just balance on a spiritual level and stay there.

When her phone rang again, she rose enough to realize that she'd been in the same position for hours, and, chances were, it may have been even longer than that. She picked up the phone and checked the screen. It was Terkel. She answered it, her tone slurred and tired.

"Are you all right?" he asked, his tone harsh.

She blinked several times. "I think so. I'm not sure exactly what happened, but it took more out of me than I expected."

"You also went deeper than most people would have on a trip like that," he snapped.

"Oh, are there rules, layers, and levels? Guess you forgot to give me those details."

His tone was sad when he admitted, "I know, and I didn't realize it, until I could feel the pull on the ethers, and that in itself was something."

"Pull on the ethers?" she asked in wonder. "What does that mean?"

"Energy being shifted in a big way. Clary was working

on healing another person, and she told me that you were out there working, and that's when I realized you were going deep, probably too deep for the kind of work that you were trying to achieve."

"And yet you were the one who told me to go out there and to see if I could find Frank."

"Did you?"

She blinked several times. "Yes, and I sent the address to your men."

"Interesting," he murmured.

"Haven't you heard from them?" she asked, sitting upright.

"I've been really busy, so I haven't checked in, and they haven't checked in with me."

"Well, maybe you should reach out," she muttered. "And, while you are at it, I'll just go back to sleep."

His tone was full of laughter when he added, "You won't sleep now anyway. You're far too curious to see if they found anything."

"They did. I just don't know if what they found is what we were looking for."

"Interesting, though I don't love the fact that everything in our world is riddles these days."

"No, I don't either. It used to be simple, you know? Do something for the government, go in, do the job, and get out. Then it got more complicated, as the government got more corrupt, and life was no longer delineated by right and wrong. Instead it became more about *How do I do this and stay alive?*" she muttered.

"I understand that," he whispered to her soul. "And it's okay. You did a phenomenal job, and you survived. That's what you have to keep reminding yourself of."

"Yet there should be more to this existence than just survival," she murmured. "A lot more."

"There will be. You've been out five years, and you've hidden for a good share of that time," Terk noted. "When you hide from your problems, it takes a little longer to adjust and to adapt."

"Yet it shouldn't," she murmured. "I feel as if we should get bonus points for having hidden."

He burst out laughing. "It never happened that way in my world."

Ashley asked him, "How is it that you're doing as well as you are, when you haven't been out very long?"

"Because I have a team," he noted. "A team who works together, a team who has held on through all this. We know that we need each other, and, because we need each other, there are no arguments about it. Without my team, I don't think we would be anywhere near as far along as we are."

"Lucky you. I didn't have that team."

"No, but you don't have to stay isolated either," he murmured.

"Says you," she replied, her tone sharp. "It's never that easy, you know?"

"No, and your own hurts have to heal before you can join up with a team like mine," he stated, "but seriously you might want to consider it. You're well on your way to healing. I just think the isolation has become a habit for you because you think that you still need to heal. However, if you look at it objectively, I think you'll find that you've already pushed past that barrier quite nicely."

"Even if I had, that doesn't mean I want to go back into anything related to this field again."

"Maybe not, but there is safety in numbers," he reminded her. "Particularly with numbers like ours. Numbers where the people are like you, and you are safe and free to be who you are."

She snorted. "Yeah? Is that the propaganda you pass on to everybody on your team?"

"So far, I haven't needed any propaganda. It's just the honest truth." With that, he ended the call.

Ashley had to sit and wonder if that were even possible. Was there a group of people who she could feel comfortable with? Where she wouldn't feel isolated? Wouldn't be alone? The answer was unclear. She couldn't imagine not feeling like the world was against her. Things worked out for her here because nobody really paid any attention to or was bothered by the strange woman at the end of the road outside of town. The few people who ever came to see her thought she was harmless.

She hadn't needed much to live on here, and she bought anything she needed locally. The only person she'd stayed in touch with was McClintock, and that was because of their history. She couldn't even imagine what it would be like to have somebody like Terkel in her world on a regular basis. He was irritating enough right now, and she knew better than to consider the prospect of his changing. She felt his laughter *whoosh* through her mind, and she smiled, trickling him a message. *It's true, you know?*

It is, he murmured back at her telepathically, *but it's a two-way street.*

She sighed because, of course, that was the truth. When you had that kind of relationship with people, it went both ways and required trust on all sides. Her solitary life hadn't required much in the way of trust, so she was out of practice and uncertain of how much she could muster. Plus, she had sworn that she would never have anything more to do with this lifestyle. *I guess I'll think about it.*

After Terkel left again, a thought popped into her mind out of nowhere. *Is somebody trying to force me back in again?*

She practically heard the gears turning in her mind. Is that what this was all about? Is that why that sick young man disappeared? Is somebody gearing up to see what she could do? And then what? Hold her captive again? Was it the government? Because she was more than done with any of that, and, if that's what someone thought they would do, they had another think coming.

She got up slowly, then walked into the kitchen. She needed food, though it didn't really matter what it was. But she definitely needed some fuel in her system. She quickly scrambled some eggs and made herself some toast with fresh bread from the village.

As she sat outside with it, she slowly started to feel some of her energy returning fully. Yet her mind and soul were confused. Plus, she was still tired and worn out, a state she hadn't felt in a very long time. That wasn't comfortable, or even something she thought she would feel again, at least not this soon.

When McClintock contacted her a little later, she was sitting outside, sipping coffee.

"How are you doing now?" he asked, his tone tinged with worry.

She smiled. "I'm better. Getting some sleep really helped."

"Is that what you call it?" he asked. "Personally it seems more like you just unplugged. It's not like sleep because it's not even that sense of relaxation and rest. It's almost a disconnection from the world around you. It's a very bizarre thing."

"You're one of the few people who's seen me do it," she noted. "So keep it to yourself, will you? It might freak out the locals."

He burst out laughing. "It definitely would freak out the locals, and I realize it's one of the things you prefer to keep to yourself."

"Good," she murmured. "Did you come up with anything?"

"Ah, that's you, right to the point already."

"Yeah, a young man's life is at stake."

"Now tell me something. Do we care about this young man?" he asked curiously, not with any emotions in his tone.

That was one of the things about him that had always drawn her. It was as if he looked at the world completely dispassionately. It amazed her, and, at this point in time, she sometimes felt that everything he'd had to do in his life up until now had eaten away at the part of his soul that allowed him to feel empathy. Or maybe he never had it in the first place. She seemed to be his Achilles' heel, and it was a real problem because she didn't want that responsibility. She didn't want that connection. She murmured. "Yes, I think we do. Remember? He came to me."

"Yet maybe that doesn't matter," he offered. "Maybe it doesn't matter that he came at all. Maybe it's better if we just wipe out any record that he'd ever been here."

She froze. "No, that would not be a good idea."

"Are you sure? Because you won't like any of the information that I found."

She winced, and her back straightened. "It's still better if I know."

"If you say so," he murmured. "Just remember that I

warned you."

"Warning noted," she murmured. "Now, let's hear it. What did you find out?"

He sighed. "I wish I didn't have to tell you, but here goes. Remember Najor?"

"Najor, Najor," she muttered to herself for a moment, and then she snorted. "Yeah, I remember him. A pencil pusher, penny pincher, or whatever you want to call him. He made our life hell because he kept cutting budgets, so we would get less and less in the way of reinforcements, less in the way of food, supplements, and all that stuff. He kept saying the government was responsible."

"Yeah, he's gone private. Beyond that, apparently he's taken to hassling some of the original people from our team."

"Oh, *great*." Ashley winced. "What's he trying to do now?"

"If he's gone private, I suspect he's trying to set up his own team."

"But why would anybody want to work with him? He had a terrible reputation. He never went to bat for us or tried to make our lives easier. He never supported us in any way that I can think of," she pointed out. "Why would anybody want to work for him?"

"I'm not saying that anybody is working for him. I'm just saying that he's out looking for people to work for him."

"The differences are slight," she murmured.

"No, they're massive," he corrected. "I don't know whether he has any ability to force people to work for him or not." At that, she sucked in her breath, as he rushed to continue. "I'm not saying that's what he's doing with this young man."

"No, but you brought it up," she said, "so obviously it's something that you've thought about. Your mentioning it already means that there is merit to the story."

"It's certainly something I've thought of," he admitted. "Hell, at one time I even considered setting up a team myself, though I would do it a hell of a lot better than Najor ever could."

She had to agree with that. "You would, and I wonder if you haven't done that because I don't know anything about what you even do. I didn't want to know. I just wanted all this to go away."

"And it did," he stated. "You haven't had to deal with any of it, have you?"

"Nope, I sure haven't," she murmured. "Was that the ostrich part of me, just sticking my head in the sand and hoping it would go away?"

"Absolutely."

"I'm not sure it was the right thing to do at that point."

"I wouldn't worry about it now," McClintock said. "It's already been a long time, and it's been a process. I'm just letting you know that Najor's out there, and he's looking for recruits."

"He hasn't contacted me, so either he knows what my answer would be or he hasn't figured out that I have anything to offer."

"Or he knows what your answer would be, and he grabbed the young man instead."

WALKER COULDN'T HELP himself and snatched his phone from his pocket and quickly dialed Ashley. "What's wrong?"

he snapped.

She hesitated. "You know that's getting very irritating."

"I don't care whether it's irritating or not. Something's wrong. Just tell me what it is," he demanded.

She sighed. "I really don't like the strong-arm techniques."

He pinched the bridge of his nose. "Then at least tell me that you're fine," he said, with that note of urgency. "I know something just hit you hard."

She sucked in her breath. "How do you know that?" she whispered.

"I don't know. I don't know anything about it," he muttered. "I can just tell that's what I felt. So, what's going on?"

"It was just suggested to me that maybe this young man was kidnapped in order to push me into doing something."

"By whom?" He put it on Speakerphone so Calum could hear. "Who would do something like that?"

"Somebody I used to work for in the government. We didn't get along very well, and I'd already erased him from my mind. He's apparently gone into business for himself and is recruiting a team, but McClintock is wondering if maybe he grabbed the young man as a way to pressure me into working for him."

"What would your answer be?"

"My answer would be no," she stated, "but, to save the young man, well, maybe …"

"Would he kill Frank to prove his point?"

"Yes, but he doesn't have … I don't even know how to explain what this guy is like. Think about somebody in the military who's always cutting corners, then runs to the boss and tattles. The guy comes back and gleefully tells you about cutbacks made because of your failures. Then you find out later, *he's* the one who made the suggestions, largely because he knew it would make us suffer more."

She appeared to be trying to reel back some of her anger by taking a deep breath. "That's the kind of guy he is, and even that didn't explain it very well."

"Oh, don't worry," Calum replied. "We get it. We've all met guys like that, the ones who were happy to rise to the top on somebody else's blood, sweat, and tears. Yet, when it came down to it, they weren't exactly the kind you wanted to have on your team."

"No, I would never work with him or for him. The last time I saw him, we had quite an argument, so, if he is involved with Frank, Najor has no love for me. The thing is, he doesn't have any love for anybody. That's just the kind of guy he is."

"So, that answers our question. If he wanted you to do something for him, he would take this young man as his hostage until he got you."

"Yeah, but why would he wait though? He's not contacted me. Nobody has," she shared. "If the young man is suffering, waiting for somebody, for some kind of a rescue …"

"Nobody even knows if Najor's got Frank," Walker pointed out.

"If Najor *does* have Frank, why would he wait?" Calum asked. "That's a very valid point. If this is what's going on, and it's still a big *if* at this point, what would be his reasons for waiting before contacting you?"

"I don't know," Ashley admitted, "but I can guess." Then she took a deep breath. "He would be waiting until the young man was as close to death as possible."

"To make him suffer?" Walker asked. "Most people

want a live, somewhat healthy hostage."

"In this case, no, because if Frank came to me, Najor would know that I was willing to help, which meant there was something I could do. That would imply there is money to be made, so he'll use the young man and his life as a way to get me to do something."

"That makes sense, but still, surely he would want a live hostage."

She hesitated and then winced. "I was able to do some healing work on Frank from a distance," she muttered.

At that, the men looked at each other and Calum smiled. "So, it worked, *huh?*"

"It did, but I'm really tired. I'm not used to this, so it's wearing me out. But the good news is, Frank is alive. I was focused on trying to keep him alive, so I hadn't looked around at any potential dangers in the vicinity. It wasn't what I was focused on at the time. I just went in to help him. I wasn't thinking somebody like Najor could be with him."

"Could you tell if Najor was there?" Calum asked.

"I don't know," she said. "I always had people around to help me, part of the team thing. Remember?"

"I do remember, and that's part of the team thing here with us too. Do you have anything you can offer from that visit when you were healing Frank?"

Her tone sounded far too exhausted as she whispered, "Can I send you guys to check an address? Frank's alive, but he's in rough shape, and we do need to find him as quickly as possible."

"Give us the address again," Walker said, "and we'll go check it out. We've just gone all through town, asking if anybody has seen him, and, so far, it's been a dead end."

"No. I don't think he went to town. I think he went to

see somebody else, another healer, either by accident or maybe he was forced. Then something happened to him on the way."

"Okay, I hear you there, and we'll be happy to check it out. Any lead right now is way better than what we have, which is nothing," Walker shared.

"Yeah, well, I'm not sure how much of a lead it is," she muttered, her tone fading quickly.

"Just give me the damn address, then go get some rest."

She snorted. "Are you always this bossy?"

"Sometimes, yeah. But then, so are you." She gasped again, and he chuckled. "Come on. We don't have time for this." She gave him the address, and he felt the sense of fatigue in her tone yet again, as she finally got it out. "Are you always this exhausted after a healing?" he asked.

After a moment she replied, "This one was unusual."

"But he's alive?"

"He's alive, yes …" she said, in between pauses, "but he's in terrible shape, and I don't know if we can keep him alive."

"We'll need to find him fast then. The sooner, the better," he replied briskly. "We'll head out right now. Are you going back there to heal him further energywise?"

"No, I can't," she whispered, suddenly distressed, her tone breaking. "This is why I don't want to do this kind of work anymore," she cried out. "I wish I'd never told Terkel I would do it."

"You told Terkel that you were delighted to have an avenue to try, weren't you? It's not as if this is Terkel's fault."

"No, it's not his fault, but it's never Terkel's fault," she snapped.

At that, Calum snickered. "We're all in the same boat when it comes to that, but Terk's very powerful, and what he knows is beyond us all. He understands us, and he knows what we can do, so he often pushes us to do more than we ever thought we could, and that's not a bad thing," he added. "He's not the government. He looks out for each of us."

"But maybe my healing Frank triggered exactly what this Najor guy wanted, which is knowledge of what I can do and that I'm still doing it. In Najor's mind, that means he can still capitalize on it."

"He won't capitalize on it," Walker declared. "We won't let that happen."

"What happens when you go back to whatever world you're in?" she asked. "No way you'll stay here and protect me forever," she muttered, "so that just puts me right back into the damn soup again."

"What about McClintock?"

"Sure, and there's always a price, no matter who it is I pay. There's always some damn price." With that, she disconnected.

Walker looked over at Calum, who was already punching the address into the GPS app on his phone. They headed back to the motel, picked up their rental, and drove off. "Any idea why she would have been so exhausted?"

Calum nodded. "I think it's probably not something she's used to doing from a distance."

"Interesting," he murmured. "And yet Cara and Clary can do that too?"

"I'm sure it's something Ashley can do. The twins may likely have had more experience with it. Ashley is obviously incredibly powerful, but, if she's never really done something like this, the extra effort required for that, on top of some very serious healing to be done on Frank, can all contribute to the burnout she's feeling."

"That makes sense," Walker said. "I never really understood all that healing stuff. I'm grateful for it, and I've certainly been the recipient of that lovely added energy trickle, but I'm not a healer and don't really understand how it works. I'm just in awe that anybody can do it, much less from a distance."

"You and me both," Calum muttered. "At this point in time I think it's an even bigger issue because of whatever Ashley's going through. She's put herself out there in order to do this. I don't know whether that was her choice or she got a nudge from somebody else, but it's given us our first real lead since we arrived."

"I guess Ashley's probably just as powerful as the twins back at Terk's base, *huh*?" Calum asked Walker.

"She probably is, though I don't know anything about that. I suspect she can probably do a whole lot more than she's letting on, or even knows, for that matter. What she doesn't realize is that I didn't come here because of the missing young man. I came here because of *a problem in Finland*, and I still don't know whether it was Ashley or Kim's brother's angst that sent me here."

"I don't think it matters who or what sent you here," Calum replied, tapping him lightly on the shoulder. "You're here, you're involved, and no way you'll convince me that Ashley doesn't matter to you."

He frowned. "Doesn't matter whether she matters or not. You heard her loud and clear. She doesn't want anything to do with us."

"That's only because things have always turned out in an ugly way for her. Maybe if we can make this turn out with a better ending than what she's expecting, she won't be quite so adamantly against it."

"I don't know," Walker replied. "That may be asking for a lot."

"All we can do is try, man." And, with that, they returned their attention to the road ahead of them. Calum looked at the GPS. "We're almost there."

"We picked up a tail," Walker confirmed. "It's most likely the ones we already met."

"Why do you say that?"

"Because it feels that way. I don't have any better way to explain it."

"You don't have to. I work on feelings too and happen to agree. What we must do is ensure they don't find whatever it is they're after."

"While they're trying to do the same thing and to ensure we don't find whatever we're after either, it's not a good deal for anybody," Walker said.

Calum nodded. "Particularly when we have no local support and no law enforcement willing to go to bat for us."

"Yeah, how does that work?" Walker asked, staring over at Calum. "Since when did it become us against the rest of the world?"

"In our case, it became that way when the government tried to kill all of us on Terk's team, including Terk," Calum declared. "We very quickly went dark and didn't depend on anybody, not even other team members. We laid low, healing to various degrees, some of us in comas. Especially at first, when most of us were still out of action. One by one, we woke up and came back to find our world had changed, and our contacts from a lifetime of doing the type of work we did were suddenly all suspect. We knew we couldn't trust anybody anymore. The risk was too great. All we had was each other, and *there* is where we put our trust—to a point I didn't think was possible."

"And yet, that is a trust that you guys have together," Walker noted. "Nobody joining the game late will have that same level of trust."

"You gain it very quickly, as we're all part of the same team of energy workers," he stated, looking over at him. "I don't know whether you're looking at working for Levi, who I know is seeking additional help, or considering coming over to Terkel's side of life with your special gifts, or maybe even stay in Finland," he suggested coyly, "but I suspect you'll find that, if you were to come and spend any time with us at all, you would feel that same sense of belonging that all the original team members do."

"It's that *belonging* that most of us are looking for, and none of us have found."

"That's true when looking from your perspective, but those of us in our group have found something we thought was impossible, which is why Terkel is opening it up as a safe space. A supportive and secure space for people like us."

"He's not exactly running a home for wayward psychics, is he?"

"No," Calum said, with a chuckle. "But, like Ashley, it's more a case of those who need to be there can find their way somehow."

"Right, and, if you don't need a place like that, you won't find it."

"That's the theory," Calum said, "but Terkel seems to know people from all over the world, and, just when we think he doesn't have a connection or we'll try something completely different, he just looks at us and smiles, then says he happens to know someone who might do a little something after all."

"Still, all of you were attacked, and all of you went down, right?" Walker asked.

"That's true, but Terkel's superior abilities gave him a split-second edge, so he was able to protect himself a little, and he didn't go down nearly as hard as the rest of us. He's the one who worked to bring us each back up and online again, and it would take another psychic or somebody who works with energy to even begin to understand how draining that can be with one patient, but with even more? It's a wonder Terk lived long enough to support all our energies in healing mode. Thankfully, each guy who came back, while not 100 percent yet, could take on some of the healing support, giving Terk a break to recharge. Meanwhile, we were starting from scratch, with no equipment or anything, still hiding from our attackers. All we really had was each other."

They took a turn to the right, per the GPS, then headed down a long driveway toward what looked like a small farmhouse at the other end. As they got out, Walker sniffed the air and smiled. "There's an awful lot to be said for rolling hills, even if there is a nip in the air."

"It's beautiful here, isn't it?" Calum stated, with a nod. "So many beautiful places are in the world, and every time I see another one, I just have to stop and take a moment."

"And yet," Walker noted, "this probably isn't the best of times to stop and smell the roses."

Calum chuckled. "No, it sure isn't. I assume you've also picked up on the fact that we're being watched, right?"

"We can pretty much count on it regardless," Walker muttered. "One thing we know for sure is that we're likely to get an unfriendly reception."

"Maybe," Calum said, "let's go find out."

As they walked toward the small house, the door opened, and an older lady, stooped over, having weathered what looked like a lifetime of labor, stared up at them. At that point, Walker realized he didn't even speak Finnish or Swedish. He looked over at Calum, who had his phone out and was quickly setting up translating any speech for them now.

The other woman looked at him and cackled. "I speak English. Not well, but I speak it."

"That's good," Walker said in relief, "because we don't speak yours."

She just laughed again, as if it were the funniest thing ever.

"We were told to come here. We are looking for a young man who has a very serious medical condition," he explained. "Do you know anything about him?"

She stared at him, then slowly shook her head. "No, I don't, and why would he be here?" She spoke with an astonished expression as she shifted, half bent over still.

It quickly became obvious that she couldn't straighten up, due to whatever medical condition she was suffering from, a fairly common affliction of the aged.

As Walker took a hesitant step toward the doorway, she looked up at him. "You're welcome to go in," she offered. "You look like soldiers."

Instantly, Calum put his hands out in front of him and shook his head. "We're not soldiers. We're not here to hurt anyone, but we were told that we might find the sick man or at least learn something about him here."

She shook her head. "I don't know why anybody would tell you that. I used to help all kinds of people in this world, but my skills are old and rusty now," she whispered. "I don't even see very many people."

"And you haven't seen this young man?" Calum pulled out the picture and held it out for her. She looked at it, then nodded. "Oh, this young man. Yes, I have seen him," she declared in delight. "A delightful young man."

The two men turned to look at her. "When was this?"

She pondered that for a moment. "Just a few days ago. He was very friendly and was looking for Ashley somebody or other. I didn't know the name, so I couldn't help, but he was very gracious and polite. Why are you looking for him? Did you say he was ill?" she asked, looking from Calum to Walker, "I hope nothing's happened to him."

"He's gone missing," Walker shared, carefully studying the older woman and looking for any sign of deceit.

She nodded. "Unfortunately that happens a lot around here. They get lost, keep walking in the dark, go over a cliff, I don't know." She gave a wave of her hand. "It's not an easy place to get lost. Yet somehow we seem to lose a number of people every year."

"Do you have any idea where Frank went from here?" he asked her.

She looked at him, then shrugged. "Oh, I didn't see him here. I saw him in town."

"Ah, okay, where in town? Because, so far, we haven't had much luck."

She frowned. "That makes no sense because he was in the restaurant. You know, the one right beside the motel."

At that, the two of them looked at each other. "We asked there today. Yesterday too."

She stared at him. "I live a simple life and don't have much money, but my great-granddaughter works there. So, when I can, I try to stop in for a lovely cup of tea, so I can spend a moment with her."

"Yes, of course." Calum understood. "What does your great-granddaughter look like?"

When she described her, the two men shared a look. "What is that look for?" the older woman asked.

"She was our server this morning," Walker said.

"Yes, of course. She's generally the only one there full-time."

"We asked her about this young man."

She stared at them, then shook her head. "You have to be wrong. She has no reason to lie." Then she paled in an instant. "Oh no. Some people in town don't like it if we talk to strangers."

"Maybe that's what happened."

"Oh dear," she whispered. "What have I done?"

"Nothing," Calum replied, as they were quick to reassure her. "We won't say anything. So don't worry."

She looked at him hesitantly. "For me, I don't care," she explained. "I'm past the age of anybody giving a crap, and they just say *I've gone round the bend* anyway," she muttered. "However, I can't have any trouble for my great-granddaughter."

"We won't cause her any trouble. You have our word. Besides, she said all the right things earlier."

"Yes, but now you'll go back and talk to her again."

"Is there any place we can talk to her without causing her trouble?"

"If you go to her home perhaps, but I won't give that to you."

They hesitated, then nodded. "That's fine. We don't want to put you in any more trouble. Did you see Frank go into the restaurant?"

"Yes, of course, I talked to him in there myself. Didn't I say that?"

They nodded, thanked her, and left, not wanting to upset her any further. As they returned to their car, Walker stopped and looked around. "Was he ever here?" he asked the older lady.

She shook her head, looking puzzled. "No, why?"

Walker frowned, as if he wanted to lift his nose and to sniff the air around him, because it felt to him like that young man was here. Or had been at least. He shut the car door he had just opened, then walked back toward her. "Earlier, you mentioned I could go inside and look around. Are you still okay if I do that?"

She frowned at him but then slowly nodded. "Yes, I am okay with that. He was a lovely young man."

Her use of the past tense bothered Walker, but he walked inside the house, recognizing a simple life, with just a chair, a table, and a few things in the kitchen that made the older woman's world a little easier. Only then did he realize the depths of her poverty or the simplicity of the life she had chosen.

Behind him, he heard Calum and the older woman talking, and Walker quickly searched, looking for whatever it was that was bothering him. When he came upon a scarf, a simple scarf, he picked it up and felt the *zing* of a connection. Almost instantly he caught a vision of Ashley holding the very same scarf. He frowned, as he walked back out to the woman and asked, "Is this your scarf?"

She looked at it and shook her head. "No." She reached out a hand to touch it, and he realized, as she brought it up closer to her eyes, that her eyesight was severely compromised.

"You don't see very well, do you?"

She shook her head. "No, not for many, many years now," she whispered, "but I don't know whose scarf that is."

"That's fine. Do you mind if I take it with me?" She hesitated again. He smiled and added, "I just want to give it back to the rightful owner."

She shrugged. "It's not mine."

"Has your great-granddaughter been here at all?"

She nodded. "She was here a couple of days ago. She does try to keep in touch as much as she can," she explained, her tone turning warm and gentle.

"What about Ashley? Has she been here?"

"Ashley who?" the woman asked again.

There didn't appear to be any guile in her tone, which surprised Walker even more. But then again, maybe Ashley knew more than she was telling him too. "Ashley Henkell. She's the healer this young man came to see."

"Ah, I heard a healer was in town. I was happy to hear it," she murmured. "I can't do it anymore."

"Is that the work you used to do?"

She gave a hard laugh. "I used to do many things back then," she said, "but not for a very long time."

He hesitated, wondering how much he could ask her about the type of healing she did.

"I need to go in and lie down if you're done," she simply said, with a pointed politeness that made him realize they had overstayed their welcome.

He stepped out of the house, smiled at her, and nodded. "Thank you."

She nodded and slowly closed the door on them.

As they walked back to the car, Calum asked, "What's

with the scarf?"

"I'm not entirely sure," Walker replied, "but I picked it up and got all kinds of visions of Ashley. I don't know why, don't know how, but, according to this woman, Ashley has never even been here, and the older woman doesn't know who she is. So that doesn't make any sense."

"Then again, she has no vision to speak of, so what are the chances that somebody was in that house and she didn't know it?"

"While she's sleeping, it's quite likely, but the great-granddaughter could easily have been there too."

"So how do we talk to the great-granddaughter?"

He looked at Calum and replied, "Very carefully because I did see Ashley when I touched this scarf. I also saw her healing the young man, and he was alive but not doing very well at all. And I definitely got a sense ... that he's not alone."

"Meaning?"

"I don't think he's the only person who needs healing in that group."

"Group?" Calum repeated, stopping at the car and looking at Walker in shock.

"Yes, group. When I say something weird is going on, I mean *weird*. I'm not just getting the energy of one person who's injured or hurting. I'm getting energy from several."

CHAPTER 7

ASHLEY LOOKED OUT the window, hearing a vehicle in the distance. She wasn't surprised when Calum and Walker pulled up out front. As they walked inside her home, she frowned at them, and Walker frowned right back. Her lips twitched. "Can't say I ever expected somebody as cranky as you to walk into my life," she muttered.

"Ditto," he replied.

She glared at him, and he just smiled, walked over, and gave her a hug. She stood stiff in his arms, wondering how long it had been since somebody had held her.

He looked down at her and said, "It won't be this way always."

"Says you," she muttered, with a shrug. "I'm still not prepared to change my life."

"We'll see about that," he added, with another smile. He looked over at Calum. "You want to bring her up-to-date, or shall I?"

Calum snorted. "Nope, I sure don't. You're the one who picked up on that weird precog and all, so you should. I can't even begin to explain it."

She looked up at him, staring intently. "What did you find out at that address?"

"I didn't find anything concrete," he shared. "However, we did have an interesting visit at that house."

"Who was there? I kept getting weird energy about it all afternoon."

"Which is also interesting because I picked up your energy there."

"I've never been there," she said, looking at him.

"That's good to know. That was one of the questions I wanted to ask."

"You're not making a whole lot of sense. Come on in, sit down, and relax. Obviously the heat has gotten to you." She looked at him crossly.

"What heat? It's freezing out there."

She laughed. "This is nothing for Finland. Besides, it helps keep us isolated. Honestly, we're happy to be loners."

"I've heard that," he muttered, "but anything can be taken too far, you know?"

She shrugged. "I'll put on the coffee." She made the statement as if it were a very magnanimous gesture.

He laughed. "Thank you."

After she put on the coffee, she returned to the living room and sat down on the only unoccupied chair. "Now, tell me what you're talking about."

"I never really got clear-cut information on anything," he muttered. "We were there, met the former healer, and I found a scarf."

When he held it out for her, she looked at it with trepidation, as if it were a snake. "I don't touch things very often," she noted, with a shrug, refusing to take it from Walker.

He stared at her, then glanced at Calum, who studied her reaction with interest. "Why is that?" Walker asked.

She glared at him. "None of your business."

"Obviously it's connected to the work that you do,"

Walker replied, "so it would be nice if we had an explanation."

"It would be nice if I had an explanation too," she snapped, "but I don't, so it is what it is."

Hiding his smile, he went on. "I think it belongs to Frank, the young man who was supposed to see you."

"Frank?" she asked, as she looked down at the scarf. "What was it doing there?"

"We're not sure about that, but, when I picked this up, I got a vision of you working to heal a young man who was suffering physically."

"That could be possible. I mean, I am working with Frank, and you know that I was working on his system remotely. Was he there at the address when you visited?" she asked, suddenly frowning at Walker.

"No, not that we could sense. I don't believe he was there. However, the great-granddaughter had been there, and she is a waitress at the restaurant. The older lady did say that she had seen Frank at the restaurant but had no idea why her great-granddaughter wouldn't have acknowledged it, except that apparently some people in town don't like it if the locals talk to strangers."

Ashley blanched, then slowly nodded. "Yes, that's quite true. We are a community of strangers, and we like to keep it that way."

"That's fine, but then when somebody comes to your community, do you not help them when they get into trouble?"

"In an ideal world," she replied smoothly, "they would never get into trouble."

"Obviously something is going on in this town that's far from ideal," Walker snapped. "Remember? Frank is a family member of a friend, and we're over here trying to find out what happened."

She nodded. "I am far more concerned about his health than I am about why you're here."

At that, Calum looked over at Walker and suggested, "You should tell her the rest."

Walker hesitated, but she eyed him quizzically.

"You picked up more?"

He nodded. "But again, it has to be taken with a grain of salt."

"That's fine," she murmured, "although I've always thought that to be one of the most bizarre phrases I've ever heard. I do understand what you're trying to say, however."

"Good, then maybe you'll understand this." He took a deep breath. "It appeared from the vision that I had, or from the energy, the reading, whatever," he clarified, with a wave of his hand, stumbling over the exact words. "From the way it appeared in my vision, it's possible that Frank's not alone."

"Of course he's not alone," she stated, staring at him. "If he is being held for some nefarious reason, yet to be revealed, he's not alone, so that's hardly shocking news."

He nodded. "I get that too, but this is different. I also got the impression that he wasn't the only one needing healing, that whoever he's with, and I don't know whether it's one, two, or however many are also injured, sick, or dying. So the question I have is, when you were doing the remote healing, were you healing Frank or were you healing somebody else as well?"

His words floored her, and she sank back into her chair and just stared at him.

"From the expression on your face, I can see that we have completely surprised you," Calum noted.

"Absolutely. … I don't know how my face looks, but, if it's anything other than shocked, that would be a surprise to me."

"There is an element of shock, but there is also an acknowledgment of sorts," Calum shared. "Even I can see it."

"I'm not saying you're right, and I'm not saying you're wrong—because I don't know. I was struggling with something, something I hadn't done before, at least not in a very long time," she corrected. "I'm not used to doing healings from a distance, unlike other people in your group, I guess. And I know that when I'm hands-on, I'm much more powerful but …" She stopped and winced.

"What?" Walker asked.

"This will sound terrible, but I was really shocked at how poorly I performed. At how much my energy was drained and how much was … I don't want to say *siphoned off* because, of course, in healing you're giving it away, and you send it out with love, knowing that it will come back to you but in a completely different way. So, I'm not trying to say that anybody was *stealing* the energy or that I was up against something along that line."

She fidgeted before continuing. "However, it seemed to drain from me at a much faster rate than I expected, and I was beyond exhausted and worn out at the end of it. And that was really disturbing because it was such an unusual state of affairs."

"So, that in itself bothered you, I presume?" Calum asked.

"Yes, of course," she replied, facing Calum. "Wouldn't it have bothered you?"

"If it's new, different for you, you wouldn't know what to expect," Calum added.

"Yet, in the past, I've done it," she repeated, "and, when I do heal, it's not as if I haven't been working on various aspects of healing over time. It's just that this time it seemed to be really … I don't know." She shrugged and shook her head. "All I know is that it was different, very different this time, and the drain was … taxing."

"What are the chances that it was because more than one sick or injured person was there?"

She looked up at him. "I'm wondering that now, if it was because more than one sick person was present. I was just sending out the energy, wrapping up whoever it was in my arms and trying to infuse as much healing energy as I could, trying to tap their minds, so that they would accept more and more and more, because I know that's part of the problem in something like this. Without the mind of the recipient being in full agreement, without the mind believing and being part of the process, it doesn't matter how much I do. He, they, it, … whatever person we're talking about here just won't heal," she stated simply.

"They may feel somewhat better, but true healing? … That takes much more effort. So, when I came back out from that, I was distressed at the fatigue I felt, but I was also wondering what had happened and why," she shared. "I didn't say anything because I figured it was just me, not used to a remote healing session. I figured I didn't have my normal healing abilities because I was upset. I hate to say it, but being a healer means coming from a space of complete and whole oneness with the world around you, and I haven't had an easy couple of days," she murmured.

"So, that session makes better sense then, if you weren't operating as you usually do, both remotely and involving more than one patient, plus the added distress in your life,"

Walker shared.

She frowned at Walker. "While I was coming to terms with the idea that it was me and my upset detracting from the healing session, now you're suggesting it may not have been me at all, and it might very well have been that I was trying to heal more than one person simultaneously, without even knowing it."

WALKER STUDIED ASHLEY'S face for a moment. "I guess another question we need to ask then is whether anybody else has gone missing recently."

Startled, the two stared at him, as Calum nodded. "I guess that's another avenue we haven't explored. Maybe this isn't so much about Frank and his condition. Maybe it's about the fact that he's come to see a healer."

Walker looked over at her. "Have you had any other clients who didn't show up?"

"No, I don't think so," she said. "I don't take on very many, as you know. They find their way to me."

"That's fine, and maybe they did find their way to you but didn't get this far," Walker suggested. "Maybe somebody is interfering in your pipeline."

She just stared at him blankly, but Calum nodded. "Right, you know we've certainly seen some crazy reasons why people do things," Calum began. "So, this could be jealousy. It could be wanting to stop something or along the lines of evil even. It could be anything, if we're considering all angles now. The problem is, we just don't have enough information."

"Right," Walker added. "So how would we find out if

anybody else has gone missing in this town, particularly recently?"

She shook her head. "I honestly don't know because I keep to myself. I don't even follow the local news."

Walker shook his head. "Do you have a news source where the townsfolk would announce or publish something like that if they aren't going to the sheriff's office with this? It sounds more likely that you guys are all about keeping to yourselves and not letting the world know if there is a problem. I mean, potentially you could have a half-dozen people who have gone missing. In fact, the older woman—the former healer at that address you gave us—said as much."

Ashley winced. "That would not be good."

"Ya think?" Walker asked in astonishment. "Friends, families, loved ones, all are waiting for people to come home."

Calum frowned. "Yet you would think, if that were the case and if other visitors have gone missing from this town, there would be some sort of investigation on a much larger scale. Family members would have reached out, trying to find them."

"Maybe it's just not time yet. Maybe these are all more *dropped through the cracks* type of people," Walker noted.

Calum shook his head. "All of that seems a bit much, considering that these missing people might also then be people who need healing," he acknowledged. "Regardless, it's something that we need to explore though. I'll contact Terkel, see if an honest lawman is in town," Calum announced, getting up and stepping outside.

At that, Walker turned and looked back at Ashley, to see an odd light in her gaze. "What are you thinking?"

She was disoriented and lost, yet her mind was working on overdrive. "You just brought up something I hadn't even considered, and I'm trying to access the energy work I was doing remotely to see if it's even possible that I was healing more than one person," she replied. "Terkel pushed me to try this, to reach out to find Frank from a distance. So my methodology was different than when I'm working with somebody up close, so it's possible I guess."

Walker added, "It's also possible that it could have been somebody who knew you would go looking for this guy and needed the healing energy for himself."

She frowned at him and then shook her head. "I think you're hitting the realm of fantasy at this point."

"That could be," he admitted, giving her a ghost of a smile. "However, to ignore the possibility won't help any of us."

She winced at that. "Fine," she muttered. "You do you. I'm still stuck on trying to consider the possibility of more than one person being there when I was healing remotely."

"It could certainly be more than one. Maybe two or more prisoners are involved, and somebody was trying to help them, and they all ended up in trouble," Walker suggested. "Just because they're missing doesn't mean that it's potentially nefarious."

At that, she gave a broken laugh. "In my world, when people go missing, that's usually enough to know that trouble's afoot."

"You're also coming from memories of working in a very broken world," Walker pointed out. "From a place where people did horrible things to each other, and you haven't had a chance to find other people who are here to help."

He left it at that, knowing she wasn't ready to hear anything else. He also understood part of what she was saying because, when you're doing the kind of work she was doing—what Terkel was doing before—you saw the worst of humanity. Walker had seen way too much himself to become complacent, and just enough was going on in the world right now that he wasn't sure he wanted to get too involved in this kind of work again. That would be one of the reasons why he wouldn't want to work with Terkel, except the whole community aspect that Calum described was definitely appealing.

When you had spent a lifetime alone with these kinds of abilities, you really did want to know if you could do more. It was intriguing to think what kinds of things Walker could do with the chance to work with somebody like Terk, who understood. Walker believed his development would be much faster under Terk, plus Walker could learn from Terk and his team, while they could learn from Walker. Not that he felt as if he had much to offer in terms of others learning from him, but it was hard to say. Calum had mentioned that being together had made them all progress in different ways.

Walker studied Ashley's face, which even now was shut down with a contemplative expression. He knew that she wouldn't share her thoughts with him right now, yet he wondered about somebody who had abilities to the extent that the government could possibly be trying to recruit her. How she felt about working for them again was a whole other story.

She looked over at him and frowned. "Your thoughts are very heavy and hard and also very loud, so could you turn it down at least?"

Startled, he winced. "Does that mean you can read my thoughts?"

"It's not so much reading, but you're transmitting, and it would take far more inducement to get me to go back to that line of work."

"That doesn't mean that somebody isn't out there looking at raising the inducement to get you back."

"That possibility has been pointed out to me," she noted. "In which case I would be very sorry for this young man, but that won't happen."

"You also need to close the healing pipeline, so nobody else can come toward you, because, if Frank *is* a victim, every other potential person out there is one as well."

She got up, walked into the kitchen, and came back with two cups of coffee.

Walker took his and looked outside for Calum, who was still busy on the phone, pacing back and forth, animatedly talking to someone. Presumably Terkel, but, since they had a whole team, and Calum himself had family, it was hard to say who it was.

Walker watched Ashley sit back down again. "Look. I know you're keeping secrets, and I know those secrets are important to you," he began, his tone low, "but, if they'll possibly hurt people, you may want to find a way to share them."

"Sharing them doesn't help," she stated starkly. "There is nothing of interest to you. Not that they're secrets really, just nightmares."

"We all have nightmares," he said, his tone simple and nonthreatening. "Sometimes it helps to share them, and sometimes it doesn't."

"It doesn't help me. I've tried. I keep hoping for peace and quiet, plus a way to walk away from all this. That's why I don't care about the healing aspect of others in lieu of sacrificing my own health and well-being, although I know …" Then she shrugged and stopped.

"You know that your soul needs you to express your gifts in order to survive," Walker stated. "Are you willing to let your soul fade away into nothing by not utilizing these skills?"

She shot him a look, and he gave her a small smile. "It's the same for me. It's the same for Terkel. It's the same for Calum. Everybody has abilities, but, if we don't use them in some way or another to the benefit of humanity, we'll shrivel up inside, and our life will become a shell of an existence—and potentially far shorter."

"Of course," she murmured. "In many ways it's a death knell to all of us, and, yes, I'm perfectly prepared to have it all dry up and go away. Honestly, for many years, I wished that such a thing would happen."

"Yet it didn't, did it?"

Slowly she shook her head. "No, it didn't. But that doesn't mean that I don't still hope that it will."

He didn't know what to say to that. It was obvious that whatever had been in her history was pretty rough, traumatic even. As she wasn't into sharing, he didn't want to push it, but the curiosity was deadly. He just had to tamp that down and remember it was her business, not his, and, if she wanted to share, she would, but only if and when she felt comfortable enough to open up. He knew they were a long way from that.

"Yes, we absolutely are," she declared, glaring at him out of context.

He sighed realizing what she'd done. "Can you at least not read my thoughts or at least read the other ones?"

"No, those ones I definitely don't want to read," she

snapped, a flush rising up her cheeks. "The fact that you're attracted to me does not mean that I'm attracted to you."

He burst out laughing. "It doesn't have to mean that, but you'll be lying to yourself if you don't read your own body's energy coming in my direction."

"Don't worry. I keep pulling it back," she noted. "It doesn't matter whether it wants to go in that direction or not. It won't go there unless I give it permission."

He smiled. "And I would never want such a thing without permission on both sides," he replied. "You are a beautiful woman, and you've obviously been broken in many ways. You've been damaged and hurt, but you don't have to stay that way. To be well enough to heal others means you've healed yourself, and any healing you do and give is to the benefit of your own soul."

"Which is why I try to heal them when they come," she stated. "I've just been doing it slowly and in my own time."

"Good. That's all that anybody can expect. Life is for living and sometimes, when the songbird is caged, they don't want to continue living. That's probably what happened to you, but there is a better life out there, and, believe it or not, you've come a long way since you arrived in Finland."

Her gaze was sharp, as she stared at him. "You don't know that. You know nothing about what I was like when I got here."

"Broken," he repeated. "That is something we can all see." She flushed at that. "No, we're not trying to look, but you have clearly come a long way because you're nowhere near as broken as you were when you got here."

"No, I'm not, and I have come a long way. And I definitely won't slide backward."

"Do you think getting involved in this will set you

back?"

"No, but only because I won't let it," she said crisply. "If there is one thing that I will do, it's protect my space, myself. For me to have any kind of a future, it's important that I find a way to live within the reality of what my current situation is."

"And yet it doesn't have to be here," Walker said, as he motioned around the room. "There are other spaces where you will be safe."

"Will I?" she asked, looking at him with an odd expression. "Can you guarantee that? Can you even guarantee that anyone who comes to my door is safe?" she asked, hysteria rising in her tone. "How can you guarantee my safety?"

He gave her a ghost of a smile. "You and I both know that we can put energy protection rings around us."

She waved her hand. "I've used those, and you really can't trust them."

"No, but, as early warning systems, they are a great avenue for staying safe. So, maybe you haven't had the right place, the right location, the right security system yet, but that doesn't mean that we can't find one for you."

She obviously didn't know what to say to that, and just then Calum walked back inside.

"Three men," he said, his tone harsh. "I had Terkel get on the phone and talk to the local mayor, with all kinds of threats about teams coming over to search, but, within the last six weeks, they've had three young men go missing here."

"What?" She gasped, jumping to her feet. "Seriously?"

Calum nodded, his facial expression grim. "Yes, and whether you knew about them or not is a whole different story, but the mayor admitted that, with this latest one, it's obvious that he'll have to get some help."

"Three?" she repeated.

"He didn't seem to think very much of the idea, but he also didn't like the idea of his budget being decimated trying to find these men."

"Yet they didn't do anything to find them before?" Walker asked.

"According to him, they have, and they run a proper sheriff's office, even though a lot of the locals are a little bit on the ornery side. It's part and parcel of not trusting strangers. Yet Terkel can be very persuasive when it comes to doing what's right."

Calum continued. "In this case, the mayor didn't necessarily do anything wrong, he just didn't do what was right. However, it may have been out of ignorance. It seems he just hasn't been in the know about what's going on here. Anyway, an investigation is being opened into Frank's disappearance, and it's been added to the list of other potential missing persons. All three are young men, relatively unknown, and nobody here seemed to have any prior relationship with any of them. It's possible they all came to see Ashley. At least that's what the mayor is wondering, since we know for sure that Frank was."

"But I don't know about the other two," she interjected.

"That's possible," Calum agreed, "but then again, you keep saying that if they come to your door, you'll deal with them, but you won't deal with them any other way."

"That's true," Ashley replied. "Yes, some people have just stepped off the beaten path to my house, without any prior warning," she added, wondering out loud, "and I definitely helped them. But, in Frank's case, he contacted me ahead of time."

"So, because you knew he was coming, you also knew he

was missing, but, with the other two, it's possible that you didn't know, right?" Calum asked her.

"Yes, absolutely." She frowned at him. "And, if I'd known that many people were missing, I probably would have said something," she murmured, getting up to head to her kitchen nook.

Calum looked over at Walker. "Are you getting any reads on her?"

"She's incredibly upset right now," he murmured. "I think, in her need to keep everybody at a distance, she quite possibly missed some early warning signs. She didn't want to acknowledge what was happening, so now we have three missing men. Why men, I wonder?" Walker murmured, with a note of curiosity.

"Most of the time women travel together," Calum pointed out, "whereas men are often the ones who travel on their own. If we have a lone kidnapper, taking out a single male is easier than taking out a couple females."

Walker nodded. Nothing to argue with that logic because it was right on. Women generally didn't travel the world alone, although certainly some trends were changing in that regard. "I wonder if somebody could be targeting Ashley, keeping an eye on her." Walker shrugged. "Or it really could be all related to her past."

"If it is related to her past, we need to find out fast because somebody is setting up hostages, if that's the case." Calum winced. "Can you imagine?"

"Why keep that many though, and not announce it?" Walker asked him.

"Yeah, especially since they're sick—if we're going with the theory that all three were headed to Ashley for a healing."

"Maybe she's not responding to some sort of telepathic

ransom message. That's another possibility that occurred to me," Walker suggested.

"What do you mean?" Calum asked, staring at him.

"What if this kidnapper knows what Ashley does and is using these people to send out an alert or warning, even maybe she had … What if this is all related to her? What if she had an early warning system on before, but she shut it down when moving here five years ago? Yet somebody is still using it. Now these three people have been possibly kidnapped as leverage and are potentially hostages to try and get Ashley to come deal with the kidnapper. However, because her system is shut down, she's not even hearing the messages."

She rejoined them, her face pale. "That," she uttered in a broken whisper, "would be horrific."

Such bitterness filled her tone that both men stood up and walked closer.

"I did have a system I used formerly," she told them, "and, yes, I did shut it down, and believe me. I don't want to open it back up again. The last person who sent a message was somebody who tried to kill me," she murmured. "I really don't want to open that door."

CHAPTER 8

A S MUCH AS she hated it, Ashley knew that explanations were needed. With a sigh, she began.

"Part and parcel to the government work that we did was, well, … not a Morse code setup but a system we worked out of sounds and beeps that we could easily send telepathically, energywise, so people would feel that nudge and would recognize either that things were going well or that there was a problem, depending on what the signal was. One of the first things I did was shut that down and hard," she muttered.

"Why?" Walker asked.

"Because it was one of the aspects that kept me up at night, even after I left the government, because it seemed like all I heard was calls and beeps, particularly after I escaped, and then again not long ago." She jumped to her feet and looked around the room almost frantically. "It was really starting to get to me. Not very long ago I reinforced that energy door, so that nobody could send or receive."

"Meaning *you* wouldn't send or receive," Walker clarified.

She slowly nodded. "Dear God, are you thinking somebody is trying to get a hold of me? Trying to get me back into the business?"

"We knew that was a possibility," Calum pointed out.

"Yeah, but I wasn't …" She took a deep breath, clenched her eyes shut for a moment, until she was a little calmer, then added, "I made it very clear when I left that I was gone for good and wasn't coming back, no matter what."

"The *no matter what* is the problem with that," Calum pointed out, "because, in most cases, people aren't willing to believe what you say, so it doesn't matter *how* you say it. If they have a need for your skills or want your skills back, some will do whatever they can to make it happen. In this instance, it's quite possible that somebody is kidnapping people and expecting you to use your abilities to save them. And maybe the first one or two were even healthier, or maybe not even looking for you, but, if the kidnapper sent out an alert, and you didn't respond, he may very well have just killed them and tried somebody else."

She sagged onto the nearest chair in despair.

Walker asked, "How many people here know what you used to do?"

"None," she said, and then winced. "McClintock," she murmured.

At that, both men looked at her sharply.

She shrugged. "We worked for the same outfit, and he's been very helpful in keeping me under the radar."

Calum looked over at Walker, who was thinking the exact same thing.

"How much do you trust him?" Walker asked.

"I trust him implicitly," she stated. "I saved his life, and he saved mine. We both retired and wanted to come here, or at least someplace where we would be safe and alone."

"Why here?"

"This was an area he knew. He was raised not far from here," she shared. "As damaged as I was at the time, I was looking for a bolt-hole. He offered me that lifeline, and I took it. If you are asking if I think he's involved in this, that would be a hard no."

"Why is that?"

"Because I don't think he would do anything to put me in danger."

At that, Calum asked, "I know you don't want to answer this, but is there anything between the two of you?"

She gave a short laugh. "No, there isn't," she declared, her gaze going over to Walker. "However, it is something he wants."

"You haven't though, so why is that?" Walker asked. She glared at him, and he shrugged. "Hey, we're all adults here. I know there's a bond between the two of us, and whether you choose to move forward with that is up to you, but, if something's between you and McClintock, it would help us to know."

"There isn't that bond between us," she stated. "There isn't that energy, but he doesn't see energy. He doesn't work it the same as I do, so, for him, that's really not an issue. He wants a relationship, and he cares a lot about me, so, for him, those two aspects are enough."

"But not for you?" Walker asked.

"Don't go putting words in my mouth," she snapped, her tone harsh, or trying to be anyway. "I can't tell you how things have come about. All I know is that he's been an incredibly good friend, and he was there when I needed him."

"And, for that, we owe him our thanks," Calum said.

She nodded. "I definitely owe him mine."

"Could he have had an ulterior plan down the road?"

"I would hope not, but, people being people, I can't say

for certain that he would never do something. I don't know," she muttered, "but I would certainly hope he's not involved."

"For the moment, we'll keep our minds open to the options facing us," Walker noted smoothly. "Now we need to just find out who else might know. Who else might have something to do with this?"

She stared at him, bewildered. "That person I spoke of before, Najor, that we all hated."

"Right, and I need to get Terkel to check on that," Calum muttered, "although he may have already." Calum pulled out his phone and sent off a series of text messages.

She sipped her coffee, feeling the heat working through her brain. The trouble was, what they said had some validity in her brain because she felt a weird sense of unease or even something being a little off. Worse than that, she wasn't even listening, and yet she'd been so sure that everything was shut down and that she could keep it that way. Instead, was it possible that other people were suffering because of her being so adamant about not helping anyone? Almost immediately she looked up to see Walker standing there, glaring at her. She threw up her hands. "You don't have to read my mind."

"I wouldn't if you weren't transmitting," he stated succinctly.

She glared at him, and he squatted in front of her. "You can't take all the blame in something like this. You know perfectly well that crazy people are out there, who do these things without a bit of care for others. You've been a victim before. You don't want to be a victim again."

"No," she declared, shaking her head. "I still struggle to live with some of the things that the military did, and some of the things I was forced to be involved in, but to think that somebody might be using innocent people to get at me now?" She shook her head and fell silent.

He gathered her into his arms, feeling her initial hesitation, as he wrapped her up and held her close. She didn't do anything at first, but moments later she finally sagged against him as he just held her. It was hard for her to let go, hard to accept the comfort he offered, hard for her to even realize that the comfort was there.

She pulled back slightly and looked up at him. "I just hid, you know?" she whispered. "I hid from everything. I couldn't handle any more and came here to lick my wounds and to hide away from society, though not society at all. It was the government. The things they did, that they wanted us to do, I just couldn't be a part of it anymore," she whispered.

"I think they knew that, and there was always that fear in the back of my mind, you know? That they would find me. I was afraid of being taken out. I knew too much. *Where the bodies are*, as they say. But that didn't happen, and more time went by, and it still didn't happen. I don't want to say that I relaxed, but it's almost as if I shifted gears at some point and went from being a hideaway mess to somebody who could rebuild a bit of a life. And I started doing more healing here and there, because, as you mentioned, if I don't heal, if I don't use my gift, … life can get pretty ugly."

"Absolutely," he agreed gently. "We all have had similar experiences, and you really need to consider spending some time with Terkel and his gang, even if only to understand that he has survived exactly what you're afraid of. All of them have, even Calum. They were all attacked by their government. They were all taken out with some energy weapon, all injured in varying degrees, some in a coma, and yet, with Terkel at the helm, looking out for them and ensuring that each of them got the support they needed, they all eventually came back online, healthy and sane. If that wasn't amazing enough, there is one more thing, and it's really important."

She looked up at him quizzically, not sure what could be more important than coming back sane.

"They came back stronger," Walker whispered to her gently. "You know what that means for us, for anybody in our situation. How cool is that?"

"Is it though?" she asked. "What would I do with more?"

He smiled, then gently kissed her on the temple. "Just think about it. You could do more with healing. Imagine if you worked with somebody like the other two healers in Terkel's group. What if you could heal people with even more devastating diseases? The results would be endless." She snorted and he chuckled. "Believe me. I know the joy, the sense of doing something positive for somebody," he shared. "That's worth so much."

"That's why I heal now," she admitted in the faintest of whispers. "Because there has to be something in this world worth living for." She gave a quick shudder and leaned back against the chair, as if trying to put space between them.

However, Walker wouldn't let it happen. He picked her up in his arms, sat down with her, now sitting in his lap. She stared at him in shock, as he burst out laughing. "It's truly been a long time for you, hasn't it, sweetheart?"

She frowned at him, hating that he could see so easily who she was.

"It's not easy," Walker told her. "I get it, but there is that connection between us. I don't know why, and I don't know how," he admitted, "but I, for one, am grateful for it. I've been alone most if not all of my life. I'm not sure I knew it, until it happened here with you, but all this time, … I've been looking for you."

When a knock came on her door, she bolted off his lap in shock. Calum looked at the door, then over at Walker. Calum held up a hand to reassure her. "It's all right. It's just Riff."

Looking up, the door opened, and Riff walked in, then took one look at Ashley standing there, ready to bolt, and smiled in a way that Ashley had never seen before.

She didn't even know Riff, or that anyone capable of such a look. It was full of caring and gentleness, as if understanding the wounded bird in front of him. "I'm not here to hurt you," he began. "I'm one of Terkel's men."

She stared at him, her shoulders sagging. "Thank you, … but a little warning would have been nice."

He chuckled. "I kind of come and go like a ghost," he admitted. "It's the way I'm happiest."

She stared at him for a long moment. "No, you feel in control of your world that way. That's why you do it."

His eyebrows shot up, and he studied her with respect. "That is very true," he agreed smoothly. "It's much easier to not feel like you're being manipulated and coerced by everybody around you, when you insist on playing the game your way."

"That's what I need to do," she murmured, studying him carefully. "I never did learn that technique."

"That's because you're a healer, and you must have your energy open in order to heal. I'm not a healer." His tone turning hard, he continued. "Like most of the team, including Walker and Calum here"—he waved a hand at both men—"we each play the game the way we know how."

Her tone hardening, she snapped, "With violence."

Walker gently picked up her hand in his. "We only use

violence as a defense mechanism," he stated. "None of us wants to screw up our own energies by hurting somebody else if we don't have to. Remember. We might not be healers, but it's still self-destructive to send out negative energy."

THE TWO MEN left soon after trying hard to get Ashley to acknowledge the issues at hand and to open up that wall of energy to see who might be trying to contact her. Riff stayed behind to keep watch outside. Walker knew she was reaching a breaking point, and, with Calum at his side, they'd both left to try to meet with the sheriff to see if they could come up with an action plan to find out what was going on. They also needed to get busy with the details of the other missing people, which apparently the mayor or the sheriff had given to Terkel, but not very willingly.

Of course nobody here in this tiny little town in Finland really understood who Terkel was, what he was doing, and what impact dealing with him would have on them. But no more time to waste. Not with that many missing. The sheriff was apparently willing to meet with them—or had been forced into it by the mayor. The sheriff's level of willingness and motivation remained to be seen, but still, it was something.

It took fifteen minutes to get back into town, and, as they walked toward the sheriff's office, they could almost sense the hub of activity in town stop for a moment, as the townsfolk assessed the fact that these strangers were not only back but they were going into the station. Calum looked at Walker with a quirky smile. "Nothing like attracting attention just for showing up."

"Right," he muttered. "Can't wait to see what kind of reception we'll get inside."

With that, they walked inside the sheriff's office. It wasn't exactly a busy place, so it was kind of silent already when they entered. It didn't take long for the two people in the front room to realize they were standing here. One woman got up from her desk, walked up to the counter, and asked what they needed.

Unfortunately she didn't speak English, but the sheriff bustled out just then. "They're here to see me," he muttered, as he waved them back into his office, where they sat down in the two available chairs. The sheriff glared at them, and both men just stared back, their faces blank, as they realized that, although they were supposedly welcome, they really weren't welcome at all.

Calum waited for a long moment, then spoke up. "We understand you guys have a problem in town."

The sheriff flushed. "Yes, and apparently it's worse than I knew."

"If you've got three men missing, then it's definitely worse than you knew," Calum stated. "I know you don't want to hear that, but we're here to help."

As the sheriff continued to glare at him, Calum shrugged. "I also get that you guys don't want or need anybody's help, but it's just a fact of life," he explained. "We have a problem, and we need to get it solved. We've got to find this young man who is quite ill and needing treatment, plus the two other missing people you've got on top of that."

The sheriff nodded glumly. "I sent over the files to your boss," he stated, barely containing his disgust. "Your boss has started to look for whatever he thinks he can find. I've organized a search of the last known locations of the one man," he shared. "I don't really know anything about the second one."

"Okay, and maybe you could send that same information to us," Walker suggested.

The sheriff shook his head. "No, if you want it, you get it from your boss. His credentials have been vetted, but I don't know anything about you."

At that, Walker gave a bark of laughter and nodded. "That's fine. We can get that information from Terkel." He pulled out his phone and contacted Terk. "You'll need to forward those files to us. Apparently we don't have sufficient clearance to get our own copies."

A note of disgust filled Terkel's tone as he responded, "Not a problem. I'll send them off now. They're a little on the skimpy side."

"Of course. Nobody even knew they were missing," Walker stated, "and now we're behind on finding them for sure. I don't know what the dates are on the others."

"One went missing last week," Terkel shared, "but, yes, we're already behind the curve on that one too. What we don't want is to have even more people go missing."

"No. I'll talk to the sheriff about potential reasons why these men even came to town, but I'm not sure he'll have any answers." When he ended the call, the sheriff was already shaking his head.

"No, we don't know why they came here. We do get a certain number of tourists throughout the year. Although I admit we have a bit of a cranky disposition where strangers are concerned, yet economic times have been a bit lean, and everybody needs money. Tourist dollars can be quite helpful."

"Right, got it," Walker said. "Is it possible that since the country is finally open for travel again that people are just getting out and traveling because they need a break?"

"That is possible, yes," the sheriff agreed. "And honestly, this whole thing could turn out to be nothing."

"Maybe so. Maybe these missing men just moved on, and it has nothing at all to do with your town," Walker mentioned with a note of snark. "Or … maybe you have a problem here."

At that, the sheriff flushed and nodded. "Either way, we need to get to the bottom of it. It won't be good for any of us if what you're suggesting is happening."

"We're not suggesting anything at this point," Calum noted, his tone soft, yet with an element that made it clear he wouldn't be led into making less of this than it was. "We can also bring in more assistance as needed."

At that, the sheriff looked alarmed, and he shook his head. "We don't need more assistance,"

"Then we better find these men and fast." Calum stood, nodding at the sheriff. "We'll go through the file and start searching on our own."

"This is an official investigation," he protested. "We simply can't have interference."

"I understand, but we must ensure that these people are found, and that'll be taxing on your resources. We're happy to lend a hand," he said smoothly, with a smile.

The sheriff was flummoxed, not knowing how to stop them from interfering, yet all too aware of the budget limitations he would face.

"Does anybody in town have a particularly violent or criminal history?" Calum asked, turning back from the doorway. "Somebody who would come to mind for a case such as this?"

The dismissive shake of the sheriff's head was immediate as he spoke. "No, and that's one of the reasons why we were so long in realizing we had a problem. This isn't the kind of thing that would happen here. We're not particularly friendly as towns go, that much is true, not in a social sense. But we don't harbor criminals who will kidnap young men, unless the men have done something wrong."

"Unless they've done something wrong?" Calum repeated slowly. "Seriously? You're surely not making these victims out to be the aggressors, are you?"

"We don't know that they aren't," he pointed out smoothly.

"Absent any facts on the matter," Calum pointed out, "why don't we keep an open mind? With any luck, we can find out what's going on here. I suggest you do the same. Let's find these men, and quickly too, so there are no long-term repercussions from their visit to your lovely town," he stated, with a note of irony in his tone. "Then we can all get back to what we normally do."

"What would that be?" the sheriff asked, glaring at him.

"We're in the security business," Calum shared smoothly. "We work in countries all over the world, and at times for various governments, more than you can count. So, as you can see, we are well suited to provide assistance."

The sheriff flushed at that. "That's all well and good, but all I really have regarding the legitimacy of your operation is a note from the mayor, stating that I was to provide assistance and support information requests from this Terkel person. We don't like interference from strangers."

"No, but apparently you don't like visitors either. Yet you say that you need the tourist dollars they bring. You can guess that, if news of people disappearing from your area gets out, there won't be any tourists dollars or strangers to worry about. You might want to consider that angle while you are sitting there, all high and mighty." And, with that, Calum stepped out of the office.

By the time Walker joined him, Calum was still steaming mad. "Interesting philosophy, isn't it?"

"Not that shocking though."

"That's true. Everybody wants the dollars the tourists bring to the local economy, but they don't want the headaches that come with tourists. They want the dollars, not the mess. They want the money, not the people. It's almost like they should just open up some sort of a fund and say, *Hey, why don't you just donate to our town but don't come here.* That's just wrong."

At that, Walker laughed. "We both know it's the same all over the world. Everybody competing for the almighty tourist dollar, then complaining about the impacts that tourists cause."

CHAPTER 9

ASHLEY GOT UP in frustration, having tried for the last hour to zone out, but, with everything churning around in her brain, it proved impossible. It wasn't helping on any level and certainly wasn't letting her get anywhere. Instead it was just driving her nuts with the possibilities. When her phone rang, she snatched it up, expecting it to be either Walker or Calum. Instead it was McClintock. "Hey," she replied, when she recognized his voice.

"You okay?"

"I've been better," she muttered. "Just not sure what the hell's going on right now."

"It doesn't sound good," he agreed, his tone darkening in anger. "Is it those two men? I can put a stop to that, you know."

She laughed. "No, it's not those men, and I don't need you to put a stop to it," she replied gently. "Thanks for the offer though."

"I would be more than happy to send them on their way," he added, his tone deepening.

"Yeah, a little too happy, I can tell."

He gave a bark of laughter. "It's almost as if you know me."

"As it turns out, I do," she said, "but, in this case, these men haven't done anything wrong."

"Are you sure?"

"Yes, I'm sure," she stated. "Listen. There has been a suggestion that more young men may have gone missing. Apparently two others we know of, one last week."

"What?"

It almost sounded as if McClintock was quite surprised, and she really hoped that was true because, if not, it would mean he knew more than he was telling her.

"Yes, and apparently the sheriff and his men are now involved."

"They certainly should be, if we've got more people missing," McClintock noted. "It's one thing if it's just this one guy who disappeared, particularly one who's sick, since he could have gone off the beaten path and died, for heaven's sake," he said in exasperation. "But if we've got three missing? That's a whole different story."

"That's all I've got for you so far," she muttered. "If you know any more, feel free to pass it on."

Then came an odd silence. "You know, in all this time you've generally preferred that I don't pass on any bad news."

"Right, and I know that," she admitted, "but now I'm starting to wonder if I was being too simplistic, too idealistic in my attempt to keep entirely out of it." She sighed. "I don't really need the details, but I can't have people going missing like this, particularly if they're coming to see me."

"Do you know if that's been the case though?" he asked.

"No, I don't know that yet, which just exacerbates the problem."

"Of course," he muttered. "The other thing is the fact that this could have nothing to do with you at all. These people might not even be missing, and the whole thing could be somebody sounding an alarm and worrying you more than you need to be."

"God, I sure hope so," she said, speaking with such force that she knew it surprised him too. "It's one thing to not want this kind of violence back in my life but another to determine what to do when it is here," she muttered.

"I know, and that's one of the reasons why I don't tell you when anything goes on in town."

"Right," she muttered, then winced, "but neither can I live in a vacuum, apparently."

"Absolutely you can," he disagreed cheerily. "You just need to ignore all this and get back to living that same life you've been living."

"Is that the healthiest way to do it?" she asked.

"I don't know, but I don't know that it's unhealthy," he argued. "The bottom line is that, as long as this is going on in your world, other stuff is happening that you don't necessarily want to be a part of. So, I've been keeping it away from you."

"Has there been anything else?" she asked hesitantly.

"Yeah, but remember that part about keeping it away from you?" he asked, humor in his tone.

"So, you're saying that there have been other incidents?" she asked.

"There will always be incidents in a town, but nothing that I would say has anything to do with you," he replied. "If it dealt with your past or mine, … I would have let you know."

She believed he was sincere. "That's good to know. I really don't understand what this is all about, but I would very much like it to go away."

"Yeah," he muttered, his tone changing. "Watch who

you say things like that to."

"Right, of course." She took a moment to collect herself and added, "You know I don't mean it in *that* way."

"That's good," he said cheerfully, "because we got out of that. Remember?"

She stared off in the distance, wondering whether she really was out of it or somebody just wouldn't let it go. "Do you really think there's any chance this is connected to Najor?"

"I don't think so, but, if it is, we'll find out soon enough. He won't stay silent, and he would contact you soon, and you can be sure he'll want something."

"How would he know where I am?"

"I don't know, but even our best efforts don't mean we've disappeared completely. It's quite possible that he found us. If you've been open to healing, and a few people have made their way toward you, it's quite possible that news about you has risen to the surface. Once that happens, nobody can keep a genie in a bottle forever. We've done well to stay hidden this long."

"Which is why I didn't advertise or let anybody know," she murmured. "I tried to help those who came because I figured they had the level of determination and drive to find me."

"And that came with its own level of danger, as you well know," McClintock murmured. "So, let's not worry about that. Let's just wait and see whether it does turn out to be Najor or somebody else is involved. Remember, though, that what's happening may not even be related to you," he repeated. "I hadn't realized three men were missing, but now that I know that, I can send out some men to see what we can find out from our end."

"Please do."

"I'll let you know," he said, and, with that, he ended the call.

She stared down at her phone and, for the first time, wondered if she really could trust him. She didn't want to think that she couldn't because he'd been instrumental in saving her and in getting her head back on straight. To really consider it right now would be a huge betrayal that she didn't even want to think about. She had no reason to even go in that direction, except for the fact that somebody was removing men, and those were men potentially coming to see her. She had asked him to keep her away from the madness, and it appeared that someone may be doing just that.

She could only think that McClintock's motive would be the fact that she had told him no, a final no, and yet she'd said that recently, not days or weeks ago, so he wouldn't have started this back then, or would he?

No matter how much she tried to shut them out, her thoughts wouldn't leave her alone. She really didn't want it to be that way, and she had no way of clearing the air, if that were the case, because to infer that McClintock was involved was to already break a trust if it weren't true. If he wasn't involved, she could imagine how devastated he would be that she had contemplated it, even for a moment. And yet nothing in her world would stop her from thinking that way because it was exactly the kind of thing that her world had been wrought with before.

So how could she not think about it?

As dusk fell, she got up and secured her door, something she had never done before. Then she went to her bedroom, sank down into the center of her bed, then slowly opened up the healing energy, tracing it back to where she had been working on what she thought was the one young man, Frank, to try and keep him alive. But this time she went in differently. Instead of just an open acceptance that Frank was there, she reached out with an intentional awareness, an open-mindedness to see what was coming.

She pulled the same thread that she had used last time, the thread that she had thought was that of Frank, the young man she had been planning on working with, an energy she had already recognized from their prior communication, so she knew that he'd been there. Whether he was still there or not, she didn't know because she had just opened up that connection and had started to work on him before. Now she was kicking herself for that same effortless connection she had made last time, made without any thought as to confirming who and what she was working with. This time she didn't have that innocence; she didn't have that same ability to ignore everything else around her. This time she was going in on a quest to figure out what was going on.

As she slowly drifted toward the energy she was reaching for, she heard something in the background, something odd. She froze as she sat here, but it was like an energetic knocking, something she had heard much of in her previous world, but not so much since she'd closed that mental door. She hadn't opened that door, on purpose, and it would take a hell of a lot for her to even consider such a move. So, just as she was trying to figure out what to do, the knocking came again in that same pattern she knew so well.

Immediately she snapped back into the awareness of her bedroom and quickly erased the pathway she had taken out there on the ethers. She didn't know whether or not somebody had realized she had arrived, but knowing exactly what that knocking was now—her prior notification system—was a whole different thing than being able to deal with it. That noise hadn't been there the last time, and that could only mean that whoever was doing this was aware that she had visited and had set up a message for her. But it was a message she didn't want to acknowledge, a message she didn't want to read. Yet how could she not, now that she knew what was there? That it was calling out for her?

She closed her eyes, shuddering, as she wrapped her arms around her body, knowing this was the worst-case scenario. She had always been aware that this could happen but had been determined to not allow it. Yet here it was. Regardless of what she did and didn't do, somebody was reaching out for her, and they were using innocent people to get there. Her phone rang, and she knew it would be McClintock. "Hello," she said, her tone slow, as if moving through molasses.

"Are you all right?" he snapped into the phone.

"Sure," she muttered, with a broken sigh. "It's the same."

"The same what?" he asked in confusion.

She took a deep breath. "I'm getting the same pinging, the same message system we used before, so somebody is definitely trying to contact me."

"Don't answer," he cried out in alarm. "Make sure you don't answer."

"I didn't, though I'm not sure that I really have a choice in the matter. Whoever it is appears to be the one who's got these young men."

"You don't know that," McClintock argued, "and, even if you do, it doesn't matter. You cannot give in to this. You'll lose everything you've worked so hard for."

The tears ran down her cheeks because she knew he was right, but how could she do anything less?

"Don't, don't, don't," he roared into the phone. "Give me a few minutes, an hour, a couple hours. I need some time to sort out what's going on."

"I know that," she conceded, "and I know you're working on it, but whoever created this mess is also working on it, and they want me to respond."

"And, if you do, we've lost the element of surprise. Right now they don't even know that you've received the message, and they're wondering what you'll do, … if you'll do anything, or if you even can. If you respond, you have nothing. Give me a little time," he begged, and, with that, he disconnected.

She sat there, wondering what a *little time* meant, when she heard a vehicle ripping through the night, coming toward her. She froze for a second and then the probes slammed in through her front door, and she recognized that it was Walker.

Even though she had locked the door, he was inside, racing toward her. He took one look at her on the bed, scooped her up, and hugged her tight. "It's okay. It's okay."

That's all it took, and she burst into tears. "It's not okay," she sobbed. "Don't you understand? It can never be okay again."

He crushed her close. "Tell me what happened," he urged, when she calmed down a bit.

She quickly explained what she had discovered.

"So, that confirms it's related to your history, right?" he asked, looking at her intently.

She shrugged. "As much as I can tell, yes. Otherwise I don't know how they would have known what my messaging system was."

He hesitated and then nodded. "Is there any chance that whoever's sending that signal is trying to use it as a distress signal?"

She blinked, as she looked up at him. "Oh my gosh. … I didn't even think about that."

"Take a minute and give it some thought," he suggested. "Is there anybody in your past life who might need help, and would they have contacted you?"

"This wasn't even a message to contact me specifically," she clarified. "Maybe *message* is the wrong word. It's more like a signal going out to everyone."

"That's what I'm wondering," Walker said, tilting her head up so he could look directly into her eyes. "Is there any chance that this is somebody in your world who's literally reaching out with an SOS, hoping that somebody out there still has the ability to receive that signal?"

She stared at him for a long moment. "And that would mean that they were here or not here?"

"You know as well as I do that they could be anywhere. It doesn't mean that they're here. It doesn't mean that they're not. I don't know, but, if somebody is sending messages, asking for help, are you really going to shut it down?"

"No, but if they're not sending a request for help, I really don't want to step into a trap either."

"It could be both," he murmured. "It really could be, but we'll need to find out sooner rather than later."

WALKER LET HER sleep in his arms, as Ashley dozed.

Each time she woke up, he would reassure her, and then she would drop off again. By the time dawn crested, he had her curled up in her bed, under the blankets, and he was phoning Terkel. When Terk answered, Walker explained, "I'm not sure what's going on. She received a very strange transmission. I got the energy, but I wasn't exactly sure what was happening." Walker filled him in as much as he could.

"So she's worried that it's a trap and doesn't want to respond in case it's someone trying to suck her back in again?" Terk asked.

After that things became fairly intense, involving multiple group conversations with Terk and his team, as they backtracked into Ashley's life, looking for anything that could be a possible clue. As far as discerning between a cry for help or a trap, they were nowhere.

When she woke up again, she looked around the bedroom with bleary eyes.

He smiled at her, then walked over and gave her a gentle kiss on her cheek. She looked up, bewildered, as he smiled and nodded. "I understand you have no idea how this relationship happened."

"No, I really don't," she admitted, her tone raspy. She cleared her throat, then shook her head. "I was doing fine alone, you know?"

He smiled. "You were doing fine, except that this mess was coming toward you. The good news is that you're still doing fine, even though it's here."

She gave him a shuttered look and then slipped out from under the covers and looked around. "When did you arrive?"

"A while ago. Things are starting to move, and we have a bunch of questions, but I was holding off on waking you up, until you had a chance to grab a little bit of sleep."

She nodded. "While you're still holding them off, make some fresh coffee, and I'll go grab a quick shower." And, with that, not even waiting for him to acknowledge her instructions, she dashed from the bedroom into the bathroom. He walked back out to the living room area and sent a message to Terkel, saying that she was awake but needed ten.

At that, Calum contacted him. "Hey, I caught a lift. I'm just coming down the driveway. I gather from the buzz on the phone and the messages flying back and forth that we have some ideas."

"We have ideas of something," he admitted, "but we're not sure whether it's a plea for help or a trap."

"Right, that's always the trick."

"Yes, the other question we have to consider is whether we think McClintock is involved and whether we want to bring him in."

"What are your feelings on that?" Calum asked curiously. "Given that you're the one who ran to her in the night, right?"

"Yeah, and she's doing better. She's in the shower now, but she's still pretty shaken up."

"Of course she is. I mean, when you put a lock on an energy door, you would think it would stay closed, but, in this case, the door keeps popping open."

"That, plus it's not anything she thought she could do."

"It's time for her history to come to the surface. I know she won't like that, but there isn't a whole lot of choice."

"I think that's why she's having a shower right now, to clear her head for what's coming. I've just put coffee on as well."

"Perfect, I brought some food too," Calum added. "I had no idea what she had on hand, so I just picked up some groceries."

"Good, I could use them," Walker muttered. "I haven't had anything to eat since dinner, and I've been up for hours now."

"I'll be there in a second," Calum said cheerfully, and, with that, he ended the call. Walker looked out the window and saw Calum making his way up the long driveway on foot. Riff probably dropped off Calum, so Riff could do some perimeter searches out there. With the coffee on, Walker brought out his notepad and took a moment to summarize the bits and pieces of information that were coming in.

They needed all of it to be confirmed with her, and that would be hard on her, especially those questions concerning McClintock. He had apparently worked with her and knew some of the same people. Still, Walker didn't really want to bring in McClintock, knowing that McClintock thought he had a prior claim to her. It would make things a little difficult if McClintock was in love with her.

If they were just friends, he might not hold Walker's relationship with her against him, but Walker suspected that McClintock cared more than he had let her know. That seemed sketchy, and, for that alone, Walker kept McClintock on the suspect list. Walker wondered if McClintock thought he could utilize her healing skills, even if she wouldn't be a part of his personal life. Would she work with him willingly or was this something he was willing to go the distance on, just to put her back into his work life regardless, since she'd refused his advances?

That seemed more confusing than it should be, but Walker just couldn't get his head wrapped around what that relationship between Ashley and McClintock really looked like right now.

Calum walked in the front door, just as Ashley stepped out from the bedroom, fully dressed. She smiled at Calum. "Hey," she greeted him. "Did you get some sleep?"

"I did," Calum replied. "I told Walker that he could come on his own."

"You didn't either," Walker protested, as he looked at the two of them. "Honestly, I didn't even think about it. I just jumped up and ran."

She nodded. "Sorry, I guess I didn't really need to send out such a weird and crazy signal."

"When you screamed, it was a signal that I couldn't ignore."

She nodded, with a small smile.

Walker continued. "What I find interesting is the fact that McClintock ignored it."

"I don't know whether he did or not," she stated, then hesitated for a moment, before she shook her head and shrugged. "You might as well know that, for a while, I had some pretty bad nightmares, and the screams were not something that anybody out here would ever hear or bother about, so I allowed my subconscious to let out all that pain into the night. At first, McClintock would call me every time in a panic, but finally he just shut it all down so he could rest, since there really wasn't any reason to panic."

"But now?" he asked curiously.

"This wasn't the same thing obviously," she muttered.

"I have to ask about the relationship between the two of you."

She looked up at Walker. "We're friends, former coworkers, but friends."

"So he helped you, sheltered you as you recovered, but

he wants more, and you've declined, meaning he may have lost the control he's had over you to some degree. If push came to shove, would he do something like this?" Walker asked.

She shook her head. "I want to say no—and really wish I could—but I've learned that one never really knows who and what is going on, so I don't know. Maybe."

CHAPTER 10

HAVING SAID THAT out loud was shocking, even to Ashley.

Seeing the surprise on the faces of the two men in front of her, she shrugged. "I don't believe McClintock has anything to do with this, but I also don't have any way to rule him out."

"Good enough," Calum stated.

Just then, another vehicle pulled up, and she looked out the window. "I think it's the man who was here last night, one of your guys."

At that, the two men walked to the window and looked out.

Calum opened the door. "Good morning, Riff. You look disturbed. What's up?"

He shrugged. "It's all quiet out in the world, and that makes me very nervous."

She looked at him, with a puzzled expression.

He shrugged. "I get senses of things that are wrong," he muttered, looking around, "and this is too quiet."

She winced. "Any idea what's happening down at the sheriff's office?"

He gave her a ghost of a smile. "Do you think they'll tell me?"

"No, I don't," she agreed, eyeing him intently. "Yet I'm

not sure that would stop you anyway, so you better just spill it."

With a burst of laughter, he nodded. "Nope, it sure wouldn't stop me, but I don't have any real intel on what's happening there. I did follow a group of deputies out to a couple addresses though. I stayed at a respectable distance, noted the addresses, and then went and talked to the people myself, but they didn't find anything on the missing people. Nobody saw anything apparently."

At that, she nodded. "At least they're out looking," she murmured.

"They are. I'm not sure how intensely though," Riff noted, with a laugh. "They didn't look as if they were impressed, either going into the houses or coming out." He looked back at her. "What about your friend?"

"My friend?" she asked, startled.

"Yes, McClintock. Where does he live?"

She winced. "He lives about eight miles from here," she murmured. "You can get there through the hills, if you wanted a decent walk," she murmured, pointing out behind her house. "He's over this crest and down on the other side."

"That's interesting," Riff noted. "Close enough to keep an eye on you, *huh*?"

"Yes," she said. "Close enough to keep an eye on me, close enough to keep me safe, which is what he has done all these years." Riff didn't say anything more. He just nodded, but she felt herself bristling at the idea that McClintock was involved. "I don't think he would be involved in this," she muttered again.

"No, maybe not, but let's make sure that we don't think incorrectly." And, with that he walked over, poured himself a cup of coffee, and, with a glance at the other two, said,

"Maybe I'll go for a walk."

Then came some sort of buzz, which filled the air, as if they were communicating among themselves, and she wasn't privy to it. She glared at them. "Stop that."

Calum looked at her. "Stop what?"

"Whatever you're doing," she said. "I can feel the weird energy around me. I'm a sensitive," she murmured. "I can sense when energy is being utilized. If you're trying to talk about him, at least do it openly so that I can hear what it's all about."

"If we did that," Riff replied, a smile playing around the corners of his lips, "you would know what we're talking about." With that, he tossed back the hot coffee, set the cup on the counter, then stepped out of her house.

She turned to glare at the other two. "I don't like him."

"What you don't like is that McClintock's trying to keep you out of certain information," Walker stated, between chuckles, "and that we all understand. But you don't know Riff, so it's too soon to know whether you like him or not." She continued to glare, not liking the sound of his logic either. "You need some food. We all do. The great news is that Calum brought some groceries."

She frowned at him. "I have food here."

"We just didn't want to overstay our welcome," Calum added, "so I picked up a little bit extra. Nothing fancy, just some fresh bread from the bakery, some cheeses, and a couple dozen eggs, in case you didn't have any."

"I am low on eggs," she admitted grudgingly. "And, if you can cook, that's even better." She stared at him almost defiantly.

"Absolutely," he murmured.

At that, Walker stepped in. "I'll do it," he offered.

"Keeping busy would be good for me right now. I'm still a little on the punchy side."

"You could also go get some sleep," she suggested, turning to look at him. "You're the one who stayed up all night. You didn't have to do that, you know?" She hated the crankiness coming through her tone, but she was hard-pressed to do anything to stop it, not when so many people were in her space and when her life had been uprooted without her say-so. The lack of control was getting to her.

As much as she hated it, she also knew that there was only one way to get through this, and that was to find out what the hell was going on. She knew these guys understood that, but that didn't make it any easier. Then she sighed. "Look. I'm sorry. I'm not trying to be a complete asshole," she conceded, "but it just feels like I've lost all my social niceties."

"You don't need them around us," Calum stated instantly. "Believe me. We understand. We've been where you are, and it's not fun."

She nodded, slowly realizing that he meant what he had said. "You guys really were attacked by your own people, *huh*?"

"Yes," he declared, with a nod, "and nothing is comfortable about that scenario. So don't worry if you don't appear to be on the friendly side," he added, with a smile. "That's not anything we're looking for."

"Yeah, *you* aren't," she snapped, shooting Walker a hard look. "Maybe you should tell your friend that."

Calum burst out laughing. "Oh my. I do like to see a relationship happening right before my eyes."

She shook her head. "Just because Walker wants a relationship doesn't mean there is one. I told the very same thing to McClintock too."

"True enough," Walker agreed, looking at her with a smile. "But you also know that the energy wasn't there between you and McClintock, but it is between you and me."

She hated hearing that because he was right, but she still had free will at this point, and she told him so.

At that, he chuckled. "As I told you, no pressure."

"Having you around is pressure enough, and you know that."

"Can't help you with that. I'll go make some breakfast." With that, he stepped into the kitchen nook, brought out a frying pan, turned on the hot plate, and was quickly cooking up a mess of scrambled eggs to go with the fresh bread and the cheese.

By the time she sat down with a hot cup of coffee in her hand and food in front of her, she realized how much of her cranky mood was probably due to the lack of food, and that made her feel even worse. "Sorry for my grouchiness earlier." She sighed and pushed back her empty plate. "I didn't realize how much I needed to eat."

"Particularly when you're burning through as much energy as you are," Calum added. "We see it all the time."

She winced. "You know, most people don't like to be referred to as somebody who's just more of the same, just like everybody else, as if we're completely normal."

He looked at her, his grin flashing yet again. "As you well know, nothing is normal about you," he replied, with a chuckle.

She wasn't sure what to make of that, but, since he didn't appear to be trying to insult her, she figured she would let him get away with it, *this time*. The thing was, he knew it too, and that smile on his face revealed he understood way more than she necessarily wanted him to, though he still wasn't exactly being insulting. She wasn't sure what she was supposed to do about it, except to let them do their thing. Hopefully she would come out of this at the other end and still be somewhat whole. "I really don't want to think that anybody I know was involved in this," she muttered.

"None of us do," Calum said, looking over at her, as he reached for more bread. "Nobody wants to know somebody who's involved in something like this, but that doesn't really give us the option of burying our heads in the sand and hoping for the best."

She sat back at that, wondering if she had done just that.

Then Walker picked up her hand in his and gave it a gentle squeeze. "We'll get to the bottom of it," he promised.

She nodded. "Hopefully soon," she muttered. "I'm not sure that Frank has much more time."

At that, Calum looked at her, his gaze sharp. "Did you pick up something else?"

"No, nothing yet," she replied, "but I need to get in there and face that demon—or whatever that message is coming my way. I have to see if I can interpret it, but, more than that, I have to send some healing energy toward Frank," she murmured. "The reality is, his time is coming to an end, and I just can't in good conscience allow him to die, not if I can do something to keep him alive."

"I know his family would really appreciate it if you did everything you could," Walker said, looking at her intently. "He really is a treasured member of a family, and, although that shouldn't matter, since everybody deserves the best treatment available, it does make a difference. I also know that their suffering would be real."

"Of course," she replied, her tone formal as she stood up, then tossed back the last of her coffee. "Keep me informed, please."

"How long of a session do you need?" Calum asked, looking at his watch.

She hesitated, then shrugged. "Honestly, the longer, the better, but I don't know what that'll mean in this instance."

He nodded. "Time to get at it, while we sort out a plan of action here," Calum replied.

Hesitating, she told them, "I feel like McClintock will be coming soon."

"Do you anticipate problems?" Walker asked.

She hesitated, then shook her head. "No, I don't think so."

"Good," Walker replied. "Now you go do what you need to do, and we'll take care of the rest."

She gave him a wry look. "You make it sound so simple."

"Sometimes it is simple." Walker got up and walked toward her, wrapping her up in his arms.

She hated the fact that her body curled in against him, knowing that she needed the comfort but not wanting to.

"You can be strong another time," he whispered. When she looked up at him and glared, he just smiled and gave her a kiss on the forehead. "Go."

"You make me sound like a child," she muttered.

"You are far from that," he declared, with a cheeky grin.

She flushed, then glared at him even more and quickly exited the room, her heart slamming against her chest, as she realized that, even though she didn't want to deal with him, their impending relationship was there in her face right now.

She had pushed off all thoughts of having a partner in

her life a long time ago; it was just too dangerous. If there were ever anything to validate that strategy, it was this mess she was in now. But Walker didn't seem to be concerned at all, as if that were the least of his worries. She didn't understand how he could be so calm, when everything was exploding all around her.

Of course that revealed a lot about where he was in life and how much she had walked away from. She didn't want to be dealing with this stuff, yet here it was. It was in her face, and she had no choice. The good news was that she had Walker to help her out, and she would take that any day. With that thought, she headed to her bed, intent on at least saving somebody out of this mess. Frank had come to her for help. The least she could do was give him her best efforts, even if it came from a distance.

"YOU GUYS HAVE moved down that pathway pretty quickly," Calum noted, surprise in his tone.

"Not really, but she was in pretty rough shape during the night, and it's instinctive to hug somebody who's hurting like that. That's all it was."

"No. I reckon it's more than that," Calum argued. "You've come further than you realize. From what I see, her walls are crumbling down around her, and it's making her more vulnerable."

"She's not happy about that either," Walker stated, "and I get it. I mean, we've all had walls, and God knows we've all had them come tumbling down at one point or another. However, in her case, it's even harder because those walls have kept her safe, not just emotionally but physically. So we're really asking a lot of her right now."

"She's asking a lot of herself," Calum reminded him.

"That's what makes a healer a healer."

"I won't say that I'm upset about it either because we sure don't want Frank to suffer," Calum added, "not if Ashley can do something for him, but we aren't sure where this whole scenario is taking place."

"Exactly, and the sooner we can find out something about it, the better."

As the door behind them to Ashley's bedroom was pulled shut, Calum asked Walker, "You got any take on McClintock?"

"Not a good one, but I don't have any motive either, at least not one that I can see so far. I don't see why he would be in the middle of this, and that's the part that gets me because there's always got to be a why. I don't see a personal rejection as being a strong-enough motive."

"I would hope not," Calum said, "because, of course, there is always that emotional … aspect too. For all we know, that could be what's driving this, but why now? That doesn't really make sense."

"What's changed?" Walker asked, looking over at Calum. "I mean, what could possibly have triggered it at this point in time? And why this way?"

"Surely there's another way to get her to give him another chance or else get so angry that she would know he was mad, at least."

"Rejection is a bitch, no matter who's dishing it out, but when it's somebody you've been invested in for a very long time, it's even harder," Walker murmured.

"It is, and that is something we have to consider."

"You go ahead and consider it then," Walker said. "My

brain is too tired at the moment."

Calum laughed. "I've got a lot of stuff to collate here that we're still running down. Then we'll leave in a couple hours to check out some of these addresses, the ones that the sheriff had, unless Riff finds anything."

"Do we think he will?" Walker asked, turning to look at Calum.

"I don't know. I'm getting such a weird vibe off that whole kidnapping thing. I'm just not sure what's going on. I don't know whether McClintock's running a con here, got the local sheriff's office in his pocket, or what. I'm not sure what the deal is, but, when we mentioned McClintock's name to our tails, they were scared. Interesting that we still don't have an answer as to who put them up to it either."

"Right, and that's another issue, unless, … unless it's because that meant we were going to tell their boss that they'd been made. Maybe they were hired by McClintock to follow us."

Calum considered that and nodded. "That is plausible, and he's not exactly going to tell us if that's the case."

"No, he isn't," Walker agreed. "I'm not so sure about an awful lot of elements around him."

"You and me both," Calum muttered. "Plus, those thugs could have been hired by the mayor or the sheriff. This town does *not* like its strangers. Anyway, you better go grab an hour while you can. I'm not sure you'll get much more than that."

With that uppermost in his mind, Walker stretched out on the couch, trying to force his mind to shut down and to let him sleep, at least a little. He'd woken up last night with such a shock, hearing her scream in his mind, knowing that she was in trouble, so he'd come running without any thought. He was still in the same clothes he had worn yesterday.

A shower wasn't in the cards for him just now, and neither was a change of clothes, but he'd had some coffee and got some food in his stomach. So now, if he could grab an hour of sleep and let all this information roll around his head, things were bound to make more sense. A part of him thought that they were making it way too complicated and that this situation was simpler than anybody understood. Yet, so far, how it all went together and what was really happening here wasn't clear. None of it made any sense, and the roundabout incessant trickle of information shuffling through his brain was driving him nuts.

He shifted on the couch, then stretched out even more and slowly let his mind go. He stirred a bit later, though it seemed almost instantly, to find himself not fully awake but staring at a vision, another precog hitting him hard. He watched the visions of Ashley and somebody she knew. Several men all stood around, talking, simply being there, not threatening, yet something was wrong, something was seriously wrong.

He started out looking for an answer, looking for a clue as to what was going on, but nothing was obvious, nothing untoward, nothing giving him any kind of answer. Yet there had to be something. Then out of the blue another person walked into the room. She turned around and smiled, and, without any warning, a bullet hit her square in the chest.

He bolted awake, not sure what he was supposed to do, but his heart was pounding, his chest constricted with the pain of the bullet, and he roared to his feet, as Calum raced to him.

"What was that?"

He gasped, his hand on his chest, sweat pouring off his brow. "Her being shot," he uttered, his hand where the bullet was. "There are men all around her, but nobody is stopping it. She turns to greet somebody who she knows, a smile lights up her face, then the bullet comes out of nowhere." Walker sank down, staring at Calum in shock. "I can't put a time or a place on it. I can't see or do anything about it," he complained, almost screaming in frustration. "What's the point of having this kind of information if I can't do anything about it?"

Calum could only nod. "I get that. I've heard it time and again from various people in the industry. Precog is one of the most frustrating abilities to have because there is no way to know when something'll happen or how it'll happen in order to stop it. But, if several men are around her, that is a clue. Do you recognize who is there?"

"I'm there," he stated bluntly. "You're there, and others are there too, but I don't know who. They're shadows with blurred figures. So, that could be the person or people who she's helping," he suggested, then stopped and reached up a hand toward Calum. "She's healing in my vision. I can still feel that warm loving energy, which is why, when she turns to see the newcomer, a smile is on her face. It lights up as if she really knows him. Like really well."

"Yet how many people does she know?"

"McClintock," he muttered, his tone low. "I can't see who it is, but that bullet? It just fires."

"You don't see anything past that?"

"No, I don't. It's almost as if ..." He tried to pull the images forward. "I don't know whether the bullets are coming back at us or ..." Then he stopped again and shook his head. "My vision literally stops when the bullet hits her chest. Anything after that is just my imagination, trying to fill in the blanks," he added bitterly. "I already know to my detriment that doesn't work out so well."

"Of course not," Calum murmured. "However, it also doesn't mean that everything you've seen, that what you're seeing is wrong. It just means that we have to be very careful. Also, it means that we do find the missing men, if that's what you're seeing."

Walker considered that and nodded. "Yes, I think we find them, and she's working on them, and then somebody is either trying to stop it or stop her or maybe one missing guy was used as a trap to get her there," he guessed, looking at Calum helplessly. "I can't pinpoint it any more than that."

"That's fine," Calum replied, "as long as we know there is a possible trap and approach it as a definite trap and acknowledge that somebody she knows and likes is looking to kill her."

"But who does she know outside of McClintock?"

"We've narrowed everything down to him, but that doesn't mean he's the one."

"No, and, as soon as she comes out of this healing session, we'll get all these questions answered."

"We let her complete that healing because of Frank, but time is running out, and we need more answers."

At that, she stepped into the room, her face pale. "More than that," she stated, "time is running out for Frank too. I've helped him as much as I can from a distance, but he's not doing well at all. We need to rescue him, and fast."

CHAPTER 11

ASHLEY HELD OUT her hands, still buzzing, then walked over to Calum and placed them on either side of his head. "I can get rid of that headache for you."

He looked at her, then shuddered, as the waves of energy washed over him.

She stepped back after a moment, and he blinked with a dazed relief. "I've had a bunch of healing done in my life because of the people I work with and the injuries I've sustained, but that was pretty amazing. I've never had a headache disappear that quickly before." He looked over at her with a warm smile. "Thank you."

She nodded, then walked over to Walker. "Sit." He glared at her, as she pointed to the chair. "Don't make me force you, now sit." His jaw dropped, and she pushed the chair up against his knees, and he sat down hard. "You haven't had any sleep, you're groggy, and now you're punchy from that last vision," she declared. "Which woke me out of my healing trance, by the way, so thanks for that."

He winced. "Sorry. Sometimes the visions are pretty strong."

"Of course they're strong. Plus, you're seeing ugly things."

"How many people here do you know?"

"I know people from the village. I know McClintock, of

course, and people I've seen in passing, a couple of my neighbors, just normal people," she replied.

"In your previous life, you've got this one man you know, Najor, but he's a pain in the ass, so you wouldn't greet him with a smile, would you?"

"No, of course not," she said.

"How about anybody else?"

"I stay in touch with one but not because of work," she added. "It's because of his connection to a friend of mine who died from work."

"Explain," Calum barked.

She sighed. "A good friend of mine, who did the same kind of work I do, was killed on the job. She had a sixteen-year-old son, and I have stayed in touch with him," she explained. "He's about the only one I would have anything to do with."

"Is there any chance that he would be the one who would come to shoot you?"

She frowned at him. "I don't know why he would." She shook her head, even as her hands worked on Walker's head. "I mean, no reason for him to shoot me. I didn't have anything to do with his mother's death."

"But does he know that?"

"I don't know," she murmured. "She wasn't supposed to be there, but they needed somebody to give them a hand. She wasn't quite as gifted as I was, and I was quite busy on something else at the time, and I wasn't expected there in time, so they swooped in and picked her up. As it was, the entire team was set up. It was a trap, and she died. So, I don't know who was behind that one. Maybe they figured it out after I left. We all grieved, and we had to move on. It was quite a few years ago now."

"But what if he didn't move on? What if the son wasn't able to, or what if he heard some information or details that weren't correct?"

"I don't know," she said, with a startled expression. "Again, I don't know why he would blame me. I had nothing to do with it."

"Except that you were the one who typically would have gone instead of his mother."

"Maybe," she agreed slowly, "but I certainly can't guarantee that would have happened. You have to be wrong. I think you're reaching, when you're going down that pathway."

"Maybe so," he acknowledged, "but we'll figure it out. You just keep coming up with information." They continued to ask her question after question, and, by the time they were done, she was tired, angry, and sad.

"Look. We've been over this time and time again," she complained. "I was part of a team of six, and it got to the point where I was just sick about my involvement in a lot of things. At first, I was cleared to go to a different program, but, in the end, I was never allowed to leave. McClintock was in the program with me, and we were both basically prisoners of the system, of our bosses, and we couldn't get out. When we finally did manage to break free, it was not in an easy way," she shared, taking a harsh breath. "We left with bad blood among all of us, and we disappeared from the face of the earth."

She took a moment to collect herself, then added, "We came here, more or less just the two of us. As far as I know, everybody else was gone and busy doing their own things. I've kept in touch with Lawson because I know Alissa would want me to. Yet he doesn't have any reason to come after me.

I can't imagine that he would. At least I don't want to," she admitted, rolling her eyes. "And I get that doesn't mean it'll happen that way. Hey, what I did want to tell you is, when I was doing the healing, before you jerked me out so abruptly, I did get another energy there and potentially a third."

"What can you tell us about it?"

"I can't be sure. It was faint, but, more important, I did get the feeling that they aren't that far away from here."

At that, as if she'd dropped a complete bombshell, both men bolted to their feet and faced her.

She threw up her hands. "What? Why that reaction?"

"Because we need to get there and fast," Walker yelled. "I don't suppose you recognized Riff anywhere."

She shook her head. "No. Why?"

"Because Riff is over there checking out McClintock's place. Remember?" he asked. "We don't want something to happen to him either."

"No, of course not," she mumbled, slowly looking at him in shock. "I wish you guys would get off the topic of McClintock being involved," she murmured. "That would really not be what I want."

"It might not be what you want, but does he have any old buildings, anyplace that he doesn't use but maybe somebody would know he has and could lay out a scenario so it looks like he's a culprit but isn't?"

She stared at him for a moment, processing that idea, and then nodded. "He has a pretty big homestead, and a business used to be there, so there are outbuildings, sheds, and things like that," she murmured.

"So close. Really? But why wouldn't I have noticed or felt it, if it was this close?" Walker asked.

"But how close is it really?" Calum asked her.

She shrugged. "Eight, ten miles, I think, driving. But walking distance? It's not that far. That's why I told Riff he could just walk over the hill."

"That's what he did, but what if somebody else had been keeping track of you and your place, using McClintock's place as a base, without his even knowing about it?"

"It would take an awful lot for him to not know something like that," she said. "If there's one thing that you don't do, it's surprise him. Security and protection is what he does. In our team, he was the guard. He was the one person who knew where everyone in our team was and kept track of all of it, all the time."

"What if," Walker asked, "like you, he put up walls to stop everybody from coming in?"

"Yeah, we both had to," she stated, staring at Walker. "What difference would that make?"

"What if he also put up the same walls, so that nobody could find him, and he doesn't know that they're even there knocking on his mental door?"

WALKER LOOKED OVER at Calum. "Do you have any locators on your team?"

Surprised, he gave a clipped nod. "Yeah, we have one who just joined the team. Langdon. He's our newest addition to the family. In terms of energy and specialty, locating is exactly what he specializes in."

She frowned at both of them. "What do you mean by a locator?"

"Somebody who specializes in telling us where to go," Calum said, and then he laughed, "although lots of people specialize in that at times."

She gave him a ghost of a smile. "Any chance of his doing it remotely?"

"I don't know. Let's find out." Calum quickly picked up the phone and contacted Terkel, asking if Langdon was there. When Langdon came on, Calum put it on Speakerphone. "Langdon, it's Calum. We have a slight problem here in that everybody was involved in something from a long time ago, and they've kept up pretty strong walls, meaning that they don't necessarily know who and what's going on, but there is a suspicion that some young men, injured or sick, are being held captive close by. Can you do any locating?" he asked. "Remotely, I mean? Is that possible?"

"I can tell you that it's up behind you," he muttered. "I don't know what I'm feeling, but there is a very strong suggestion of *up and over*. Does that make sense?"

"Oh, it makes more sense than you know. Thanks. Give us about an hour, and we may contact you again.'

"Listen. I can continue to text as I get information," Langdon shared, "as long as you stay on your phone and stay together. Once you split up, that doesn't work because I won't know who it is that I'm giving directions to."

"Good enough," Calum replied, getting to his feet. "It'll probably be just me heading out."

"No," Ashley said.

At that, Walker looked over at Ashley.

"I'm coming too," she declared. When he hesitated, she shrugged. "If they're hurt and are in need of healing, I'm the one who can do something about it. Also, McClintock won't throw as much of a fit if I'm there."

"Are you sure about that? This is the first confirmation we've got that he might be involved."

She gave him a dry look. "Confirmation because somebody says *up and over*?" she asked.

He shrugged and gave her a ghost of a smile. "And what happened to the part about maybe somebody's using his place, and McClintock doesn't know? Remember what it was like when you worked, when you trusted implicitly?"

Her frown was immediate, and she gave a nod right back. "That's another reason why I need to come," she stated. "I can't take the chance that McClintock will get violent if it's just you guys."

"Fine, can we drive there?"

She shook her head. "No, he does have barriers up for that."

"Interesting," he murmured. "*Up and over* it is then." Not that anybody had any idea what that would mean except her, but Walker was more than ready to do what needed to be done in order to put an end to this. And, after he was packed up, he turned to look at her, as she put on her hiking boots. "Are you sure about this?"

She gave him a look.

"Right, not to mention the fact that he's your friend."

"He's my friend, and I trust him," she said.

"And you trust him because he's always been good to you."

"Of course. That's how trust works," she stated, staring at him. "I get that you're still looking at him as a suspect in this and that I couldn't confirm that it *wasn't* him, but I'm not ready to throw him under the bus."

"Good," Walker replied. "That means, when it comes to a relationship between you and me, you won't do the same thing to me." Then he tossed her a big fat grin and walked out, leaving her gasping in his wake.

CHAPTER 12

A SHLEY GLARED AT Calum, who was trying to hide his grin and failing, as they stepped out the door. She muttered. "Is he always like this?"

He shrugged. "Oh, I've never seen him like this," he admitted. "Honestly, as far as I understand, he's been completely against having a relationship. So obviously he's feeling something he can't walk away from."

"Doesn't mean I can't walk," she muttered, glaring at Walker's back, as he walked strong and steady in front of her.

"I think he also understands resistance, and that sometimes it's useless, particularly when a strong bond is there."

"Yeah, but, just because there's a bond, doesn't mean I will act on it," she stated, knowing that, as much as she wanted to, she still wasn't sure she was ready.

"No, and sometimes we're never ready. Sometimes we just do it anyway."

She stiffened and then relaxed.

"It's still your choice. Don't feel as if you're being pressured into anything, but you should know that the connection between you is obvious. I can see it from a mile away," he told her, with a smile. "But, again, that doesn't mean you have to act on it." And, with that, he nudged her to pick up the pace a little bit, as Walker was a little farther ahead of them than he liked.

"Maybe," she muttered, under her breath.

"Maybe?" Calum repeated.

She contemplated this relationship on the horizon, as she headed to McClintock's place. It was so much harder to sort out her feelings with all this other mess going on. She didn't want to deal with it right now, but she knew that everything would come to a head, once this scenario was over. That was the first time she had admitted there *was* an end coming toward them, and maybe there was. She just didn't know how it would go. If it ended badly, it could impact her and her future in a bigger way than she really wanted to acknowledge, but how could it not?

If McClintock was involved, it had the power to hurt her at a very deep level. If he wasn't involved, and he was just as much of a dupe as everybody else, that was a different story. It was beyond her to think about it, not when all this was going on, yet that voice in the back of her mind wouldn't be silenced.

Calum continued. "Maybe? That's an excuse, another excuse, and you know perfectly well there is a potentially great relationship here for you with somebody who is already on your same wavelength, someone you already know and have acknowledged as special. You're just scared. Scared of what you'll find, scared of what might happen, scared of the future. Isn't it time to stop being scared?"

She shuddered, a physical movement that brought a concerned look from Calum. She smiled and shrugged it away. "I'm fine. Somebody just walked over my grave."

She had said it so lightly, as a way to knock away his interest in the relationship discussion and to focus it on something else, but he still stopped and looked at her.

"You know, in our world, when somebody says that …" He stopped, and she was not sure why.

She stared at him. "When somebody says that, … what?"

"I've been operating with a very specific team, and we say things that are probably very different from your team. It generally means that energy is moving, and that somebody is out there attacking somebody else."

"There's always somebody out there attacking somebody else," she stated, trying hard and failing to keep the bitterness out of her tone. "I think that's one of the things that I struggled with the most. The never-ending brutality of this world that we're supposedly protecting."

"And you're not alone on that," Calum agreed. "A lot of us have the same issues."

"What about him?" She nodded toward Walker, who still strode ahead, his gaze ever searching the forest around them.

"Him too, but he's the one who recognized what was going on over here—from America. He's the one who contacted Levi, and that's how we found out about Frank."

"Just out of the blue like that?" she asked.

"I don't really know," Calum admitted, "but, once he started getting these visions that wouldn't leave him alone, he knew he had to do something about it."

"It was either do something about it or go mad," she said, filling in the blanks. "Yes, I know, been there myself at times."

"But you're not a precog, right?"

"No, I'm a healer. However, once you know that somebody needs medical attention, and you don't help, you're withholding the care that somebody else could use. It almost becomes a crime on an energetic level because you're refusing to give them what they need, and that is devastating. For a healer," she added, with a hard finality, "it's like turning against everything you believe in."

"Yet people do it," he reminded her.

"Usually when they're forced to or when they're in a position of having to choose between one or another as to who gets to live or die, which is one of the worst scenarios." Her tone broke, even though she tried so hard. She stopped for a moment and took several deep breaths.

"Apparently I touched a nerve."

Walker looked back, then stopped to see what the problem was. He called out to them, "You guys okay?"

She took several more deep and calming breaths. "Yes, just having some rough memories."

He frowned at her, and his tone was harsh when he asked, "You let someone die?"

She blanched. "Wow, you don't pull your punches, do you?"

He winced. "That wasn't a precog though, was it?" he asked, his gaze searching, as if looking for more information.

"No, that was my history. Far too many dead or dying, and I couldn't save them all. I tried hard, until I collapsed. McClintock pulled me out of there, and, at that point in time, we lost several of our team."

"That was the last thing you ever did for your government?"

"It was," she confirmed. "I got out of the op gone bad, fought even harder to get totally out of the government, and basically told them I had burnt out at that point."

"Oh," he stopped, then looked over at Calum.

"Why? What difference does that make?" she asked.

"Because, if somebody realizes that you are no longer

burnt out, that you have healing abilities again, that changes things."

"No, it doesn't," she stated. "I would never work for them again."

"Unless you are forced to, … the way you were before," Walker stated pointedly.

She blanched and then nodded. "Even then, I can't. I mean, being connected to those people when they died, it was brutal."

"Did you know them?"

She nodded slowly. "They were my team members. One was a healer with whom I worked very closely, and another was a kidnap victim who had been shot. All of them had been shot," she said, with a wave of her hand. "If I had been closer to the team, I might have been able to save both of them, but I wasn't," she whispered. "Honestly, I haven't been the same ever since." Then she glared at him. "Does that make you feel better?"

"No, of course not," he said, looking at her gently. "Yet it does help explain some of this."

"It doesn't explain anything," she snapped. "There is no explanation for this."

"Yes, there is, and I highly suspect that what we have is somebody in the government trying to see what your abilities are, particularly now that you've been brought back into the business."

"I haven't been brought back into the business," she argued, staring at him in shock. "I won't be."

He looked over at Calum, who nodded. "You might not want to be, but, if somebody else is willing to be that much of hard-ass and not care about people's lives, as he kidnaps more and more people, that person will do whatever is needed to bring you back into the fold again." Walker took off once more.

Calum asked her, "I presume you are a very strong healer?"

She nodded slowly. "I was. I only heal now, as I told you, only when I have to or when somebody comes to me because I know then that they really need it and that it's meant to be. I don't do that high-level healing every day anymore."

"Why is that?"

"Because it takes too much out of me."

WALKER KEPT JUST ahead of them, close enough to hear the conversation but not so close that he was impeding their progress or his ability to keep searching. When they finally crested the hill behind her place that separated her from McClintock, Walker stood and surveyed the valley around them. He murmured to her as she approached, "You picked a hell of a place to isolate yourself."

She beamed. "It's beautiful, isn't it?" she asked, her tone soft with reverence.

He gave her a crooked smile. "Mother Nature is always beautiful, but also brutality is here."

"There always is. Nobody said Mother Nature was a wimp," she declared, with spirit. She pointed up on the other side of the little rise. "He's down there."

"Good enough." Walker looked over at Calum. "I'm thinking we should split up."

"Got it," Calum agreed. "I'll head down in this direction, and you stay with her." And, with that, he quickly scooted down the hill, heading to the left.

Walker watched his progress from the shadows, keeping Ashley ever-so-slightly behind him.

"Do you really think a problem is here?" she asked.

He shrugged. "I'm not sure. What I can tell you is that we were told to stay together in order to get the assistance that we needed, and we've just chosen to split up." He gave a wry look in her direction.

"Right, so how does that make any sense?" she asked.

"I'm not sure it does, but I do think we need to scout out this area."

She frowned at that. "I still can't believe McClintock would have anything to do with this."

"I'm not saying he did," Walker stated, looking at her, "but I also don't quite understand what he does here."

She winced. "He's a bit of an enforcer, not that anybody here really needs it, but, because he's always here, the sheriff's office may have a pretty easy job. When McClintock stepped in, he made it clear that nobody was to touch me, nobody was to have anything to do with me, and we had one or two incidents, and that was it. Once everybody else realized he was here, he became this big hidden threat in the background. He never had to use any force, and just one look from him was enough to keep most people in line."

"So, was that his job when you were out on missions?"

"He was a guardian," she murmured, with a nod. "A protector of sorts. He was supposed to keep an eye on me and to ensure I got to and from the jobs safely."

"And that didn't always work out, is what I'm hearing?"

"I mean, it worked out as much as it could, but nobody can be 100 percent *on* all the time, and we were betrayed once from within," she shared, with a shrug. "That changes the odds, and I am sure you understand there is little you can do about it, at least the first time."

"Ah, it seems there's a lot of that going around."

"There was, and it seemed that, for a while there, everybody was doing their best to screw everybody else over, and you didn't know who could be trusted anymore," she murmured. "It was pretty depressing, and I hated it. I hated everything about it. Yet I also knew that, to get us out of there, I would have to pull some strings on my own," she stated, with a wince. "When we had a nasty op go bad, both of us took the opportunity to change our careers, so to speak," she declared, with a hard smile.

"And what? Up until now they've left you alone?"

"Yes," she said, with a look at him. "Absolutely. Since then, it's been quiet, and I slowly healed and came to terms with a lot of my past. ... I can't fix some of the things I couldn't fix, and I haven't been able to help nearly the amount of people I used to, but it is what it is, and I can't do anything about it."

"Of course not," Walker agreed. "I still feel as if you aren't telling me part of the story."

"Maybe there are parts of the story I don't really want to discuss," she stated, her tone cool.

"Got it," he muttered.

"Nobody should be interested in what I do anymore," she said, with another shrug. "I'm not really even sure what I can do, to be honest."

"But you don't really know that, right?" he asked. "According to what Terkel and Calum are saying, everybody came back stronger. He mentioned it to me specifically."

"But they're part of a team," she pointed out. "Abilities generally grow faster in a group, than if you're alone."

He nodded, not saying anything to that.

She gave him a hard look. "I don't think I like what you're thinking."

He gave her a gentle smile. "That's okay. You can get used to me thinking it."

She shook her head and turned her attention back to what was going on around them. "I want to go down there," she said suddenly.

"Yeah?" Just then his phone buzzed. He pulled it out and saw a text message that simply read **Left**. "Looks like we're going left."

"That's where Calum went," she noted.

"Yeah, and this is coming from Langdon."

She shrugged. "In that case, let's go left."

And, with that, they turned left and headed down the hill, staying to the trees and the shadows. "I feel like I'm creeping up on a friend, and I don't like it," she snapped, her tone low.

"You can explain it to him afterward and tell him that we forced you."

She snorted. "It's not as if he'll believe that."

"Why not?"

"Because it takes a lot for somebody to force me to do something."

"Yeah? But you're also worried about people being hurt right now," he murmured. "So that's hardly a fair assessment."

She didn't say anything to that, and they continued to scoot their way down the hill. When they were about two hundred yards away, his phone buzzed again.

He pulled it out, checked the message. "Now we're to go right."

Startled, she frowned at him and then turned to face right. Almost in a perfect line was the centered view of a large shed. She walked toward it steadily, staying to the shadows, as Walker kept scouting the area around them.

"Do you trust this Langdon guy?" she asked him.

"Terkel does," Walker replied. "I'm not as familiar with anybody on the team, but, if Terk says that he's solid, we have no reason not to follow."

"Unless he's setting us up."

Walker didn't say anything to that because, if it was another betrayal from within, it would be fairly complex and complicated in order for it to involve Langdon, who was the newest member of Terkel's team. Yet Walker could see where she was coming from, considering her history. As they reached the side of the building, he pulled her back into the shadows and whispered, "Stay here."

She grabbed his hand. "I'm coming with you." He looked at her and frowned. She shook her head. "No, I'm coming. You're not leaving me in the background like this. If people are in there, I need to be in there."

"Sure you do," he agreed instantly, "but you don't need to be there if bullets are flying."

She gave him a half smile. "You and I both know that, if your vision comes true, it'll come true no matter what you do."

"That's not true," he argued in a harsh whisper. "We can change this."

"Can we?" she asked, staring at him wistfully.

"Yes," he declared. "You just have to want something past this. You plan for a life past this."

She hesitated, then reached up and scrubbed his cheek. "I could, if we ever get to the other side of this."

He pulled her toward him, gave her a hard kiss, and said, "Hold that thought. It just might keep you alive." And, with that, he quickly disappeared around the shed, leaving her standing here, glaring at the space where he had been standing.

CHAPTER 13

ASHLEY HATED BEING left behind, and she hated waiting. She understood Walker's need to protect because she'd been up against it time and time again with McClintock. But, when bullets were flying, she was the one who could do something about it. Although, exactly how much she could do that, she didn't really know.

She stared down at her hands, wondering how much value she even could offer anymore. She did healings, and, when the patients came to her, she did what she could, but was there more she could do? Was there more she wanted to do? After you've been hurt so much, it's hard to do anything except hide away in a huddle of misery and try not to believe that the world is better off without you. But, when you're a survivor, and everybody else around you has gone on doing things that you could never even begin to live with yourself, it just becomes one of the hardships of being a survivor. Yet this scenario made no sense to her, unless, as they kept saying, somebody was waiting to see if she was using her healing abilities again. That would have been a long game.

She'd been here for five years now, and that just brought to mind that, maybe up until now, the idea hadn't even occurred to anybody, until all of a sudden people started showing up here, and that meant one of her patients had talked.

She wasn't sure how that would happen. Yet it could have been an innocent conversation, as simple as somebody just saying they would go see a healer. She knew that her reputation had started to build. She had even talked to McClintock about it, wondering if it was time to relocate, but he'd been adamant that he could protect her. And so far he had, but she was beginning to realize that his protection might have carried a bigger cost than she was prepared to pay. Not that he would ever hurt her, but maybe he had done something to keep others away, something that would have hurt those *others*.

With her mind still puzzling through it, she peered around the corner, but nothing was there. It was completely calm, silent even, and that was disturbing in itself because it made no sense. Where had Calum and Walker gone? Had they been taken prisoner? Even if that were the case, what was she supposed to do here? She sank back into the shadows a little deeper from where she had been standing, waiting for Walker to return to her, when she heard a voice inside her head.

She shifted to the side, wondering who she heard. It wasn't Terkel, and it wasn't McClintock, not that he had that ability. Was it Walker? There was a tinniness to it, as if coming from a long distance away. But it was hard to decipher anything. She crouched against the building, hidden as much as she could be by the space she was in, then closed her eyes and opened up her senses. Almost instantly, a voice slammed into her brain, and a laugh broke through her mind. A hard tone.

There you are.

She opened her eyes and bolted to her feet, finding a man staring at her. He was young, possibly twenty or so, she wasn't even sure. "Hello."

He just smiled. "This is even better than I could have wished for." He chuckled.

She stared at him. "I don't know anything about this. What's going on?"

"Ah," he replied, "it's a fine time to pretend innocence now."

Then she noted his handgun.

He motioned for her to move forward, his added push causing her to stumble in the direction he wanted, as she moved toward the front entrance of the building.

"Who are you?" she asked. "What are you doing here? This is McClintock's place."

"I know whose place it is," he said, the handgun nudging her spine. "Hurry up. We don't have much time here."

She didn't even know who he was. "Who are you?" she repeated, suddenly feeling an odd push, an odd energy push.

"It doesn't matter who I am. At least it never mattered to you." She twisted to look up at him again, but he snarled and snapped in her face, "Turn around."

She turned around, but that one look hadn't helped. She didn't know who he was. "I'm supposed to know who you are, but I'm sorry. I don't."

"Yeah, and how would you? I never sent you any pictures, and my mother never did either."

She froze. "You're Lawson?"

"Yes," he said. "I'm Lawson. And you are the woman responsible for my mother's death." He shoved her inside the building. It was a huge metal dome-looking construction, and her eyes struggled to adjust. She could see one man chained against the wall. She raced over and dropped in front of him. "Oh my," she whispered, spinning to look at

Lawson. "What have you done?"

He shrugged. "It worked, didn't it?"

"What worked?" she asked.

"It brought you in," he replied.

"You could have just come to my house," she stated, staring at him. "Why didn't you?"

He looked at her almost in a fury. "Because you were too well hidden."

She blinked at that. "I see," she murmured. "You didn't need any healing, obviously."

"No, of course not," he spat, with a wave of his hands. "What's that got to do with it?"

She didn't say anything because her guards had kept out anything and everything that was dangerous to her, and only people who could heal were allowed in. Then, with McClintock's extra protection on the same level, Lawson hadn't been able to access her, until he drew her out.

She sighed, as she straightened. "What do you want from me?" she asked, staring at him, trying not to see where Calum and Walker were.

"I want vengeance," he declared.

And her heart sank at that. "Because of Alissa's death, which I had nothing to do with?"

"You did have something to do with it. You chose not to help her."

She shook her head. "It's not that I chose *not* to help her," she clarified, knowing that the guilt even now choked her. "There were too many dead and more dying. I had to choose who I could try to help who might live afterward."

"That's right, and you chose to let my mother die."

"I chose to let her die because she was already so far gone." She tried to explain, hating the note of desperation in her tone. "This isn't all that simple to work out when you're in the field, when everything blows up and when people are being killed all around you. Your mother was dying, and I can't go retrieve somebody from the other side," she stated, glaring at him. "Do you think I haven't carried her death on my heart all this time?"

"All this time you were talking to me as if you had nothing to do with it. I only found out recently that you were the one out there to heal them, and you chose not to heal her!" he cried out in fury.

"I didn't choose *not* to heal her. Too many dead and dying that day, and there was only one of me," she cried out in pain. "What am I supposed to do when I can't heal everyone?"

"You choose those who you care about. Anybody would have."

She blinked at him. "There were always too many of those," she whispered. "This was my team. All of them were members of my team. They were all dying, Lawson. What is it you wanted me to do?"

"I wanted you to save my mother!" he roared. "Up until a couple months ago, I thought you had done everything you could, … until I found out differently from your old boss, when he contacted me to see if I'd ever talked to you about what happened."

"So, that's what he told you?" she asked, the pain slicing through her.

"That's what he implied, yes. Did he come right out and say you were responsible? No, but he did say that you were a healer, and you didn't choose to heal my mother?"

"I didn't choose to heal her because I *couldn't* heal her. She was far-too-badly injured. Do you think she didn't know that? Do you think she didn't tell me to go help the others? That's exactly what she did because she knew it would have taken everything I had to try to keep her alive, but, even then, I wouldn't do it. In the meantime, anyone else I could potentially help would die. Do you think we both didn't know that?" she cried out at him, feeling the pain of betrayal all over again.

He stared at her, not wanting to believe it.

Lawson needed somebody to blame, and Ashley was it, whether she liked it or not. Her own boss has thrown her to the wolves yet again. She stiffened and glared at Lawson. "It doesn't matter whether you believe me or not, Lawson. But how dare you drag other people into this bout of vengeance of yours and hurt them too? They did nothing to you and had nothing to do with your mother's death, yet here you are, hurting them and risking their lives."

"Just one. I figured I needed just one to draw you out, but it didn't quite work that way. It was much harder than I thought. You were just totally okay with his not making it to your appointment. Like who does that?" he asked, staring at her, as if that were yet another nail in her coffin. "What kind of a person are you who doesn't care when somebody doesn't show up for their appointment?"

"What do you mean?" she asked in bewilderment. "For all I know he didn't arrive, or he was taking a few more days to travel, or was doing something else completely. I mean, it's hardly as if I'm sitting here, waiting intently for people to show up so I can work with them," she explained. "Honestly, I would just as soon not have anything to do with people, all because of things like what you're doing right now. You get a little bit of information from someone with ill intent. Then suddenly you figure you know everything there is to know, and you're all about judgment. Instead of accepting that there are things that we just can't do in this life, people we just can't save, you're sitting here, hurting more people in order to make a point. And I don't even know what point that is, since I can't go back and save her. I can't do anything."

The color on his face went from red to purple, and then all shades of anger.

"If you want to kill me, go right ahead. Do you think I haven't felt that guilt, that horror, and that pain all these years? So, if revenge is all that's in your heart, go ahead and shoot me."

The silence that fell in the huge room spoke volumes.

She looked at Lawson and nodded. "Now, at least let me see how badly injured this man is."

"He's not injured," Lawson whined. "I didn't do anything to him."

"No, but he came to me for help, and he was already on the edge of what he could survive. But that didn't matter to you, as long as you got your pound of flesh, and somebody suffered." She shook her head, then walked over, grateful when Lawson didn't try to stop her. She didn't know what his game plan was at this point, but she highly doubted it would be so easy as allowing her to walk out of here.

She dropped down beside the man who appeared to be almost comatose and reached out a hand to his forehead. She bowed her head, searching for the thread of energy that would tell her the state of his health and how severely his system had deteriorated. She reached out to Clary and to Cara, asking if they could help this young man, who had come to her and had been taken captive instead. She felt the energy stirring on the ethers, when her arm was jerked back, and she was pulled away from him.

"Leave him alone," Lawson yelled. "It'll hurt you more to watch him suffer, so I'm good with that."

She stared at him, seeing that same selfish pain and torture that he put himself through, and the guilt. "You couldn't have saved your mother either, Lawson," she whispered. "There was nothing any of us could do."

"If I'd been there, I would have saved her," he snapped.

She gave him a sad smile. "No, you wouldn't have, and you couldn't have. She took two bullets in the chest, right in the heart, and she bled out in my arms. There was nothing to be done. Can you imagine what that's like? To know that this is what I do? That this is what she did? She was a healer too."

"And when she needed healing, you weren't there for her," he cried out.

"You are wrong. I *was* there for her, in the only way that I could be. I held her while she died, as she whispered to me not to waste my healing energy and to go help the others. I got reprimanded for taking so long in making a decision to help other people because I held her," she cried out, tears in her eyes. "I was told off because of all the things that I should have done instead. There was nothing I could do for her, and she died way too fast, though it was a good thing since at least she didn't suffer," she declared, straightening up.

"So, if you want to make me suffer, that's fine. Go ahead and make me suffer. I really don't care," she yelled. "There's nothing you can do to me that my government did not already do," she snapped. "But if you think that watching this young man die is of equal value to you, then you're a sick puppy, and I hope they put you down like the dog you are."

His eyes widened at that.

She nodded. "You expect me to have all this sympathy and compassion for you now? No, sir. I'm running a little short on that these days. There was no need for you to hurt somebody else just to get back at me. You could have found another way to get your revenge. You didn't have to involve somebody innocent like this. Somebody who's already struggling to find any pathway forward in life. You just wanted to find somebody coming to me so you could make him a pawn in your world," she declared loud and clear. "What about the other men?"

"What other men?" he asked, with a smile.

She winced. "You killed him, didn't you?"

"I didn't kill anyone, but someone died here. Yes, he's buried out back."

"McClintock didn't even know?"

"He knows I'm here visiting. Don't forget I stayed in touch with him too."

"He didn't mention it," she stated, her eyes widening.

"Of course not. That's a guy thing," he stated. "I didn't want him to say anything because I knew that it would trigger you."

"No, it wouldn't have. I would have assumed that you reached out for the same support and connection that you had reached out to me for in the first place."

"Yeah, well, McClintock confirmed that you were the one who didn't choose to help my mother."

She shook her head. "The language you're using tells me that you're taking the information you were given and interpreting it the way you wanted it to be, which has *nothing* to do with the truth," she murmured. "You are overcome with rage and guilt and anger and loss, but, instead of dealing with all that, you're lashing out at innocent people, and that I find hard to forgive."

"What? You mean, I'm not broken enough for you to work on?" he asked mockingly.

"I can't fix mental problems." She glared at him and then walked over to where the young man was and sat down beside him again. "Go ahead and do whatever you'll do. I don't care."

He stared at her in frustration. "You should care. It's what you're supposed to do. You're supposed to care about people."

"Yeah, and then they turn out to be complete shits," she declared, looking at him in disgust. "You don't care about people. You don't care about anybody but yourself, about your own agenda, about what you want, instead of what other people need. You don't care about this young man. He's simply a means to an end. You didn't care about the one who already died either, and, once one death happens, it's so much easier to watch another one, isn't it?"

He shrugged. "It was kind of traumatizing when I realized the other one was dead," he admitted, "but I didn't kill him, so it didn't matter."

"Withholding care and holding somebody captive while they die alone out here is the same thing," she stated. "You murdered him, as clear as night and day, and that's how the law will look at it." She glared at Lawson. "How do you think this makes your mom feel right now?"

He shrugged. "She's dead and doesn't know a thing, and that is all because of you."

"No, it isn't because of me, but no point talking to you anymore," she spat. "So, I'm just going to sit here, close my eyes, and rest. It's been a very long couple of days." And she proceeded to do just that.

WALKER WAS STUNNED at Ashley's aplomb, at her ability to literally just close her eyes and lean back in such a dicey situation. Then he realized that her foot was touching the young man, Frank, and she was sending energy to him, trying to help him survive through this ordeal that he'd been put through. As long as she kept up that connection, she was willingly giving up her energy to help save him.

Terkel whispered in his head. *Both the healers here are working on Frank too*, he murmured. *However, we need to take out Lawson.*

Terk, I still can't be sure if McClintock is involved, Walker whispered right back.

Calum's gone to get him. We don't think he's involved, but this is on his land, right under his nose.

How does that work? Walker muttered.

Boundaries, guards, barriers, Terkel reamed off instantly. *You get relaxed after a while, thinking that it's okay. Then you don't even check your systems to confirm they are still functioning as intended*, he murmured. *You can't blame McClintock for this.*

As much as he wanted to, Walker knew it would just put him in the same category as the young man in there, staring down at Ashley with the same frustration and fury he had before. *Lawson doesn't know what to do with her*, he murmured.

No, and she's completely detached from it all. If she dies, she's okay with that, Terk added. *That's the thing about a healer. They do what they can do, knowing that they're doing the job that they intend to do here, while they're on this journey of life. Then, if they die in the process, they die in the process. There's a fatalistic air to it,* Terk explained, trying to calm down Walker. *I've come across it several times.*

It's wrong, Walker snapped.

Terkel murmured, *It's not wrong, but it's definitely not easy. She's likely to need help in order to get out of this.*

She doesn't want help. She keeps pushing people away.

She was *pushing people away, but she seems to have turned a corner on that too.*

That's when he remembered the kiss they had shared earlier. *Maybe, but I think she feels horribly guilty about everything that happened to her friend Alissa and the fact that Ashley couldn't help her.*

Of course, Terkel agreed, with sadness in his tone. *We're always haunted by our failures, and we forget to remember our successes because, in our world, there's always another potential failure happening around the corner. We try to learn from our mistakes, but the mistakes can be devastating enough that we get tunnel vision in order to avoid repeating them.*

Terkel's words just rolled through Walker's head. He understood them, but it didn't pertain to what was going on right now, except for the fact that Walker was really concerned about the way Ashley just sat there, completely detached from the world around her.

You might also want to consider that it's not that she's got a death wish, as much as she has infinite trust in those around her, Terkel mentioned suddenly. *Because, while she is in there working, she's also expecting us to do our jobs and to save her. That takes a lot of trust.*

Walker sat back on his heels at that, silent for a moment.

I guess it does, doesn't it? And it's also a sign of her willingness to grow and to move in this crazy world, and the fact that she's left it this way is huge.

That's right. Now where is Calum?

Calum is here, and McClintock's on his way. There should be a showdown happening very soon.

Any way you can throw a protective shield around her? Terkel asked him.

He snorted at that. *I'm a precog, remember? And I've already seen how this turns out.*

Such bitterness filled his tone that Terkel reacted immediately. *Stop it. That's only one possible ending, as you well know. It isn't how it does end. It's how it* could *end.*

With that, Walker stared at the tableau frozen in front of him, as McClintock stepped in through the door, his huge frame filling the doorway, as he glared at Lawson.

"What the hell are you doing?" he roared.

Lawson turned the gun on him. "Just shut up. The only way to deal with you people is with bullets." And, with that, he fired once. McClintock took the bullet in the side, and it jolted him backward, but he didn't drop. It was enough for Calum, who'd come in behind him to jump to the side, a handgun of his own drawn, as he fired a shot himself. But Lawson was no longer there, he was sitting behind some machinery, and now it was once again a stalemate.

Lawson laughed. "I don't care if I die in this," he shouted menacingly. "I really don't give a crap. At least then I'll spend time with my mother. And I'm determined that you all get to come with me. It's an open invitation, and the next one who shoots me is dead!" His tone cracked with emotions, as he roared.

"Even me?" McClintock asked, his tone hard. "This is

what you came here for?"

"Yeah, it sure is. You were just a means to an end, just as my mother was a means to an end for you guys."

"Your mother was an incredible healer," McClintock yelled, "and I was half in love with her myself. I would have done anything to keep her alive, but we couldn't. I don't know how you managed to get this so wrong, but we couldn't save her."

"You didn't try," Lawson yelled flatly. "So you have no idea whether that is even the truth or not."

Walker realized there would be no talking to this young man at all. Walker quickly dashed around to the back of the building, crept in around the machinery through the open door in the back, then shifted forward, silent as ever. He knew perfectly well how this could end.

Just like Terkel had said, Walker was willing to do everything he could to change that ending to something that was a whole lot more positive and far less painful, for him too.

"Come on, Lawson. You know better than that," McClintock called back.

The conversation welled around Walker.

"What I know is that because you couldn't care less, you let her die!"

McClintock's tone was weary. "You're never going to believe the truth because you don't want to believe the truth, and, for that, I'm sorry, son. This is not how I ever wanted things to go for Alissa's son."

"Oh, stop the bull," he snapped. "You really don't give a crap about me. You guys came here and holed up, with all that money, all those resources, and here you are, hiding away, as if you're afraid that somebody would discover your secret. I did find it, and I'm here to ensure that you both pay for what you did to my mother."

The fact that he was still going on about his mother and couldn't accept commonsense explanations made Walker wonder just where the young man was at mentally, but it wasn't the time to be working on that. He tossed a glance toward Ashley, but her eyelids were closed, and a pallor crossed her face, and he realized she'd slipped into a deep healing coma to help whatever was happening with Frank on the ethers.

A weird buzz filled the air now, and Walker knew that more than one person was working hard to save Kim's brother. Walker stepped closer to Lawson, and, when a sudden noise came outside, shots rang out, but Walker also instinctively knew that the shots hit nobody.

At that, Lawson laughed. "Do you really think you'll take me out like this? That's not helping, and it'll never happen."

"How do you envision things ending here, Lawson?" McClintock asked, his tone revealing the effects of the bullet wound.

"It doesn't matter. It just doesn't matter," he yelled, his tone tired. "I came here because of my mother, to see justice done." At that he lifted the handgun again, just as Walker came into sight. He watched as Lawson turned his gun toward Ashley. "If nothing else," Lawson continued, "I'll make sure that this one goes for what she did."

Immediately he pulled the trigger, but, before the bullet hit Ashley, it slammed into Walker, as he stepped directly in the path. He looked at the young man for a moment, then slowly dropped to his knees and fell to the ground, half on top of Ashley's legs. He heard gunshots, both in his head and outside his body. He was confused by the voices and the screams of anger, fury, and pain.

So much pain, and then he knew nothing.

CHAPTER 14

A SHLEY WAS JOLTED out of the healing buzz that she was deep into, as she worked hard to save Frank. When another energy slammed into her legs, and she felt the pain searing into her own heart, as the other healers whispered, *Go help him.*

Walker was hurt. Her energy surrounded him, wrapped him up in a bubble, and she worked to stop the bleeding. A bullet had gone in just above his heart, and even now his lungs filled with blood.

She cast an assessing glance over at Frank, but the twin healers were working on him, trying hard to save the young man, even as Clary sent energy Ashley's way, and together, with the three of them working on two bodies, with one slowly dying and another quickly dying, Ashley wasn't sure that success was even possible.

It was Alissa and that showdown all over again.

It doesn't have to be like that, Clary whispered in Ashley's mind. *We can do this.*

Ashley closed her eyes and bent down to the task at hand, a need that happened in an instant with no warning. You never have time to prepare for this kind of thing. You just start healing and heal now. But the urgency was there, and the need to save somebody's life was present.

She lost track of time; she lost track of her surroundings.

She didn't even know who was here and what happened to Lawson and whether he was even out there and still a danger to her and to these men. She didn't care. She just wanted to focus on healing Walker and being with the other healers, working on Frank. Ashley sensed the other two women at her side, working just as hard and feverishly as Ashley was, trying to save everybody. It was an interesting experience because she'd never had such strong healers beside her, and these women were good. That didn't mean that they would be good enough, but, hey, they were all giving their best efforts.

When it looked as if they were finally starting to turn the tide, Clary whispered to Ashley, *Talk to him, Ashley, and see if you can get him to pull his own healing energy into this, so we can ease back slightly.*

She contacted Walker mentally, telling him to wake up and to listen. He groaned, the pain still racking his body. *I know you're hurt,* she whispered, *but we're working on you, trying to save you. I need you to trigger your own healing mechanism to give us a hand, so that we're not having to pull on it quite so much.*

She knew he probably didn't understand the words or the methodology. That didn't matter. She just needed his permission to get his body to work with them, instead of against them. When somebody went into shock like this, it was all too easy for a body to shut down because they were already at the point of thinking that it was too late.

Sure enough, that's exactly what was happening.

"Save yourself," he murmured, his tone faint and barely above a whisper. "Lawson's still a danger."

"I don't know whether he is or not," she replied. "I'm not paying any attention to what's going on around us. All I want to know is where your mind is at. I need to know that you're here and that you'll fight this."

After a moment of silence, he whispered, "Is there anything to fight for?"

"Yes, you're alive. That's already huge."

"I'm dying," he murmured. "I don't even feel the pain right now."

"That's us. We're holding that pain at bay, so you can work with us." She sensed him struggling, trying to understand what was going on, then she smiled, leaned over, and, in spirit form, gave him a gentle kiss along his face.

"You need to live," she whispered. "I didn't fight this long to stay alive myself, only to lose the one good thing to come into my life in the last five years."

A ripple of laughter filled the energy around her, as he whispered, "Fine time for you to decide that I'm worth fighting for."

"You *are* worth fighting for," she whispered. "However, now you have to decide if *I* am." She surprised herself with that, and his response came back, soft but clear.

"Of course you are," he whispered, love in his tone. "I didn't even know I needed you, until we met," he murmured, "and now I don't know how I can live without you."

"Ditto," she said, equally softly. "That means you need to live. You need to fight and to give us every bit of help you can in order to make this bleeding stop."

"Even then, there's no hospital, nothing close by."

"Yeah, well, maybe we won't need a hospital. Three of us working on you," she told him. "I'm not saying we can pull a miracle out of a hat, but this is what we do."

He gave a soft, gentle sigh. "If you can save me, please do," he whispered. "After I finally found you, I don't want to lose you now."

And with that, she chuckled. "I don't intend on losing you, and, if I do, I'll probably just follow you anyway. For all I know, we've both been shot, and we're both sitting here in the same otherworldly plane."

"In that case," with that same gentle smile and care in his tone, he whispered, "let's both just float away."

"No way," she argued. "I want everything possible in this life. I haven't even lived yet. I haven't had a chance to have a life, like everybody else. I need that, and I want it."

"You've got it," he said, slowly turning to open his eyes and to stare up at her. He blinked several times. "I don't even know where we are or how this is even possible," he murmured, looking around.

"You're in a very different state, not quite out of body, but it's similar," she murmured. "I'm keeping you at bay from the pain that's racking through your system, while we heal as much as we can. I'm sure that somebody has sent for an ambulance, and, wherever we are, there'll be some medical professionals coming to help."

He just smiled and closed his eyes again.

"You stay awake," she snapped.

His eyelids flew open. "Am I awake?"

"You are in this in-between plane, and I need you to stay that way. Stay strong, and don't you dare give up on me."

"I wasn't planning on it," he said, staring lovingly at her. "I have too much to live for now."

"Damn right," she declared, with spirit. "But I do need to know that, if I disconnect from you, you'll still be there."

"Do you have to disconnect?"

"No, and I might not," she said, "but, if I don't, our lives will be forever bonded."

"Sweetheart, they already are," he said gently. "The moment I met you, I already knew that bond was there. I'm not sure where it formed or if that is something we came into this world looking for, but I do know that we are already all-in. Therefore, we are already one." And, with that, he drifted into a peaceful sleep, while she continued to work on him.

When another voice slipped into Ashley's mind, it was Clary, as tired and as exhausted as Ashley was. Clary said, *He's turned a corner, and it looks like he'll make it. We have to move him now.*

At that, Ashley slowly pulled back and looked around. Frank was breathing on his own, his body calm, and somewhat at peace, but she felt the twin energies vibrating around him. He had some kind of a weird cancer, and the twin healers were still working on him.

As for Ashley, she was whole but lying in the same position, with the other men standing there, glaring at her. She opened her eyes and glared right back. Then she caught sight of McClintock holding his side. "How bad is it?" she asked.

He shrugged. "Pretty minor compared to everything else," he muttered. "Lawson's dead."

She winced. "God, how did that go so wrong? I'm sorry."

"I am too," McClintock said. "I guess that's what happens when we put up the walls and keep them up, isn't it?"

"We kept them up too high, too strong, and kept everybody out, but then we couldn't see the enemy when he came at us," she murmured.

Calum crouched in front of her. "How is he?"

"I think he'll live," she muttered, fatigue in her tone, "but he's not out of the woods yet."

"The ambulance is here, and we need to move him

now."

She reached out a hand, and he helped her to her feet. "I need to stay with him," she said urgently.

"That's fine. You're going in the ambulance with both Frank and Walker. McClintock is going in the second ambulance."

And, with that, she was assisted into the first ambulance, where she sat at the far end. The two men were loaded quickly beside her, and she placed a hand on both, bowed her head, and continued to work. She still sensed the other women, healing on the ethers, as they were slowly and carefully moved to the hospital in the nearest city. The trip was long, but, with Ashley there and holding on, Walker and Frank would hopefully make it.

By the time they made it into the hospital, Ashley's fatigue was evident. When they opened up the ambulance doors and quickly removed both men, she was left sitting here, staring out at the world around her, wondering what had happened.

That's how Calum found her a few minutes later. He hopped in and helped her out. "You need to rest," he said.

"How is he?" she asked, looking at him. "Is he alive?"

"He is. They took him straight to surgery to remove the bullet. Initial reports are positive, given that there was minimal damage. They're not sure how he got so lucky."

She beamed at that. "That is great news. What about Frank?"

"They're running a bunch of tests and working on him, but they're not sure what was wrong in the first place because he's not showing signs of any particular illness. We've contacted Kim for details to confirm whatever we can do is being done, but, according to the doctors, there isn't really much they can do but offer supportive care. Apparently he is worn down, malnourished, and dehydrated from being held prisoner, but otherwise he appears to be fine."

She catalogued those words, and then nodded. "None of those are a threat to his life."

"Not at this time, no," Calum agreed, with a smile. "So, whatever the three of you did, you did well."

"I'm so glad to hear that," she murmured, then she stretched. "Can I go in and see Walker?"

"No, he's probably still in surgery. What you really need is to get some sleep yourself."

"That's not happening," she declared, looking at him. "He'll still need some healing."

"I get that. We're trying to find out what room he'll be assigned to, so we can get a cot in there for you. When he comes back from surgery, he'll be taken to that room."

She cataloged that information, then nodded slightly. "That would work. I really could use a chance to collapse for a bit." She took one step, and a second, then suddenly looked up at him and whispered, "Sorry."

She went down hard, unconscious in his outstretched arms.

WALKER OPENED HIS eyes and looked around. An odd buzzing was in his head and his body, but it was tolerable. It just felt like an irritating machine running somewhere nearby. He rolled his head from side to side but found no machinery—nothing. Then he looked down to see a hand holding his, with Ashley at the end of it. He squeezed her fingers gently and whispered, "Are you awake?"

She lifted her head groggily, then stared at him.

He smiled at the confused and drowsy look in her eyes. "Hey, you want to fill me in on what happened?"

She blinked and shrugged. "No, I don't even know what happened. Obviously something did because we ended up here." He stared at her, as she smiled. "Let me call Calum." With that, she placed a call, and with the phone on Speaker, she said, "Calum, he's awake."

"Hey, Walker. How are you doing?"

"I've been better, but honestly I'm feeling remarkable—considering."

"You mean, considering you got shot in the chest? Yeah, I would say you're doing all right. Listen. No worries though. Everything is over with, and we're all safe and sound. McClintock has been treated too."

"Good, and I presume he wasn't involved?"

"Nope, it was all Alissa's son, Lawson," Calum replied. "Unfortunately he was killed in the melee."

"I hate to say it, but maybe that's for the best at this point. He had some serious mental problems."

"It makes it nice and clean. That's for sure."

"Where are you?"

"I'm back home with my family," he said cheerfully. "You're expected here in a couple weeks as well."

"Really? Is that a thing?" Walker asked.

"Oh, it's a thing all right because Terkel wants you to come work with us."

"Oh, well, it'll be a while before I even think about working."

"Maybe so," Calum agreed, "but there's a space for both you and Ashley, whenever you're ready."

Walker looked at Ashley to see her nodding. "That's an

interesting turn of events. I'll need a couple weeks to get on my feet though."

"Yeah, I'm sure you will," Calum confirmed, with laughter in his tone. "Take care of yourself now, … both of you." And, with that, Calum ended the call.

Walker looked down at Ashley. "It's really over?"

She nodded. "Yep, it's really over. I thought …" She hesitated, and he stared at her quizzically. "I thought maybe you would be interested in spending a few weeks at my place first."

"I certainly don't have a problem recuperating there," he said, with a growing smile. "I definitely don't feel as if I'm ready to head back to work anytime soon."

"No, you'll need some time," she said. "I figured that would give us a chance to get to know each other."

"I'm all for that. Hell, yes!"

IT TOOK A few days, but when Walker was finally released, and Ashley arranged a ride back to her cabin, where groceries had already been delivered, she helped him into the living room and onto the couch. It was quiet outside. "Sorry that the trip took a bit longer than I expected," Ashley told him.

"It's all right," Walker replied. "I'm feeling remarkably good, you know, … considering."

"Yes, but that whole *considering* thing is significant," she noted. "You were shot, and your body had a lot to deal with."

"Yeah, but I have a guardian angel beside me," he said, as he stretched out on the couch. "That makes all the difference in the world."

She nodded. "I still feel bad though. You stepped right into that and literally took a bullet for me."

"I know, and I'm glad," he declared cheerfully. "I would do it again too. That vision as it was shown to me was way too hard to watch. I couldn't let it come true."

"No, but I'm not terribly impressed with your methods to alter that vision."

He chuckled. "Too bad, it's already a done deal. Plus, there is no way I could have healed you, had you been the one to be shot."

She shrugged at that comment. "How about some food? Are you hungry at all?"

He nodded. "Something light would be good, and then maybe a nap." That's what they did, and, by the time he got into her large bed and rolled over onto his side, he was out cold. She quickly had a shower, curled into bed beside him, and promptly fell asleep herself.

CHAPTER 15

OPENING HER EYES, Ashley found Walker staring at her. She flushed. "How long have you been awake?" she asked, yawning.

"Long enough to appreciate the woman beside me," he said, his tone deep and rumbling.

She reached up an arm, snaked it around him, and hugged him gently. "It still feels weird though."

"What? Waking up to somebody studying your face?"

"Absolutely," she stated, giving him an odd look. "I haven't slept with anybody in a very long time."

"I, for one, appreciate your abstinence," he declared, with a smile. "And that part of your life is over with because I plan to be with you."

"Are you sure?" she asked. "I'm still a little uncertain about going to work with Terkel."

"I don't think work needs to be part of it, if you don't want it to."

"I'm not sure that work *can't* be part of it though, since they do know I am doing healing," she stated.

"And that intrigues you, doesn't it?"

She winced and then nodded. "How could it not?" she asked. "It's who I am."

"Exactly, and that's Terkel's point. He really understands that we are who we are and that we belong over there, even if it's not necessarily where we thought we would ever go."

"You were talking with Levi about working with him, weren't you?"

"I was, but I think the problem is that people like us end up with Terkel, because, well …"

"That's where we belong."

"Exactly, but it doesn't mean we can't do jobs for Levi, if he's shorthanded, but my base would be with Terkel. I think he would be a better fit."

"Good," she said, "that makes it easier."

"It does." He hesitated and then asked, "Are you okay to move?"

"I really am. I came here to heal," she shared, "only to realize that healing was one thing, but I hadn't ever stopped hiding. I really think it's time to come out of the shadows."

"I'm glad to hear that," he said gently. "As long as you're happy to live in the sun with me, I'm always there."

She chuckled. "I can't think of anything better."

"I can," he declared, his gaze warming. "I can think of something much better right now."

Her eyes widened, as she understood his meaning, and she whispered, "You're still healing."

He flashed her a grin. "That just means you have to go easy on me."

She raised up on an elbow and frowned at him. "You surely can't want to have sex right now?"

He looked at her, his gaze that of wide-eyed innocence, and replied, "Hey, I'm a guy, and that means anytime is a good idea."

She leaned over, kissed him gently, and murmured, "It's definitely not a good idea."

"Yes, it is," he argued, as he gently rolled her onto her back and kissed her passionately, until she lay quivering beneath him.

She peered up at him owlishly. "How can you turn my brain to mush like that?" she asked. "It's really not fair."

He laughed against her neck, as he kissed her soft skin. When he came up against her T-shirt, he had it gone within seconds.

She stared down at her completely nude form and laughed gently. "Wow, I didn't know it was that easy."

"It's that easy," he confirmed, as he pulled her closer, tucking her under. He spent the next few minutes gently stroking her soft skin. "You do know that we were made for this, right?"

"We were made for each other," she whispered, feeling the tension curl deeper, as her hands stretched around to explore his beautiful male body. When she came up against the bandage and frowned, she was brought back to Earth.

But he shook his head at her. "No, I'm fine, really."

"But it would be better if you weren't this active."

He smiled. "Some things heal much better at this level anyway," he declared. "You and I both know that."

"That's an excuse," she scolded. "Anything to give yourself permission to go ahead and do this." The corner of his lips twitched, as he kissed her into a melting puddle again, and she sighed. "Fine. Apparently I have zero ability to resist you."

He kissed her again and again and again, ever-so-gently, giving her time to argue, but finally she was done with the arguing and wrapped her arms around him and pulled him close.

"Just make sure you don't hurt yourself."

"I won't," he whispered, as he slowly moved over and above her, holding himself on one shoulder, even as she sent energy into the arm to give him as much support as he needed.

He smiled. "Now that's another way to do it."

She shrugged. "I can't help myself. I'm a healer," she said, with a chuckle.

"When I'm fully healed, we'll make love with our energies entwined. I hear it enhances everything." And when he slowly slid inside her, she shuddered, her body already warm and welcoming, stretching to receive what she hadn't realized was missing, until all of a sudden it was there waiting for her.

She sighed with quiet joy, as he settled deep inside and slowly started to move. With her helping to set the pace, and her energy to keep him from hurting himself, he finally came apart in her arms in a gentle, slow, and loving way that brought tears to her eyes. As his big body jerked for the last time, her own responded with a release that swept through her and left her gasping.

As she lay here afterward, curled up safely in his arms, he whispered softly, "You all right?"

"Better than all right," she declared, tilting to look up at him. "You still should have waited."

"No way," he argued. "No way in hell I would wait any longer for that." He leaned over and kissed her soundly. "But I might just need to go back to sleep for a little while again."

"Then sleep," she whispered. "I'll look out for you."

He held her close, and his response almost broke her heart. "Believe me. I trust you to look after me anytime. Just make sure you trust me too."

"If you notice, I've already trusted you with the most important thing. I trusted you with my heart, so there is nothing else but the two of us, together forever."

EPILOGUE

TERKEL LOOKED OVER at Celia. "How many rooms do we have in this place?"

She burst out laughing. "It seems like hundreds, but we will obviously need to get more bedrooms ready and the plumbing updated in some of the other wings. Still, we have plenty of room for Ashley and Walker."

"Besides," Calum noted, as he looked over at them, "you wanted a big team, a team we can draw on, a team who could handle having families and being a part of this. So we definitely need to find room for them."

At that, Cara walked into the room, her belly clearing the way in front of her.

Terkel looked at her and sighed, as he remembered yet something else, as he asked Celia, "Did we get any forward movement on people to help with day care?"

"Not just people to help with day care, but we'll need … probably two nurses to work full-time," Celia replied. "Plus, we now have a new chef for the kitchen, so Mariana can relax a little more, and we hired more full-time kitchen staff as well. They'll come back and forth, leaving us at the end of the day, which I think is better."

"I like that too," Terk muttered. Just then his phone rang. He looked down at the screen and frowned. "Jonas, what's up?"

"What's up is that I have another job," he barked, his tone grim. "Not exactly sure if this is your thing though."

"Even if it isn't, that doesn't mean we can't do it. We just have an extra edge on the market for something geared to our particular skills."

"It's time-sensitive."

"It always is. What's up?"

"We had an Eastern Bloc specialist coming over to England, and she's been kidnapped," he stated.

"Was she moving to England?"

"She was born over here, which apparently made the decision easier for her, but her parents emigrated to Russia, and she was raised over there. She has traveled fairly extensively throughout the world, but the Russian government decided she's too dangerous to let out, that she knows too much, and she's way too skilled to let the Western world have her, so we worked hard to get her free. To our dismay, she's just been snagged out of Belgium," he shared. "We're still trying to get details, but I need a team, and I need that team now."

"Got it," Terk replied. "What doctor is this?"

"It's not just the doctor herself. It's her daughter as well."

"The daughter was kidnapped too? How old is she?"

"She's twenty-six. She worked with her mother and apparently has some of the skills that you guys have. That's another reason why the mother was trying to get her out of there because the Russian government was starting to make noise about keeping the doctor and her daughter there for their own secret programs."

"Of course they were," Terkel muttered, with an ugly

frown. "I need details, but I've already got somebody who can go."

"Good," Jonas said. "Glad to hear you're getting more people. I wouldn't have thought you had such a large pool to draw from."

"This is someone who contacted me a few days ago. Obviously I have to call and confirm, but that's my problem, not yours."

Once he disconnected from Jonas, he quickly dialed Reid. When Reid answered, Terk announced, "I've got a job for you, Reid."

"Good, I was getting a little bored."

"Where are you?"

"Switzerland."

"You're heading for Belgium," Terkel declared, and he mentioned the microbiologist.

"Oh hell," Reid replied, "that's Veni's family."

"Veni?"

"Yes, her name is Venialla, but she goes by Veni."

"You already know her?" Terk asked.

"We met years ago. She and I belonged to a large group involved in psychic work," Reid explained. "Like me, she popped in to see if she found any people like her. The two of us connected way back when, but I don't think very many others in the group had any real psychic skills. If I had thought there were, I would have told you about them already. So, in the meantime, she was looking to head back to the Western world again. I wasn't sure if that would work out. I lost track of her about eight months or so ago."

"Guess what? She resurfaced with MI6, trying to move her and her mother back to England, but now they've gone missing."

"Okay, I'm on it. Send me the deets. I'm already packed up, ready to go."

This concludes Book 5 of Terk's Guardians: Walker.

Read about Reid: Terk's Guardians, Book 6

Terk's Guardians: Reid (Book #6)

Reid Cocheran is eager to see Venialla again, after losing contact years ago when they were in the same research group. Finding out that MI6 lost her and her mother in a secret operation, while moving them both back to England, has him volunteering immediately.

Veni Baronov and her mother were caught escaping Russia where her mother, more prisoner than employee, had been working for the government. This was their one chance at freedom—before her parents' employer discovered there was more to Veni than she wanted them … or anyone … to know.

Veni had always been independent, but sometimes a little help is needed. This time it will take a lot of help, especially now that MI6 had failed them. There is someone she can call on for help, but it requires skills she didn't dare use—not when others want to wield them against her …

Find Book 6 here!

To find out more visit Dale Mayer's website.

https://geni.us/DMSReid

Author's Note

Thank you for reading Walker: Terk's Guardians, Book 5! If you enjoyed the book, please take a moment and leave a short review.

Dear reader,

I love to hear from readers, and you can contact me at my website: www.dalemayer.com or at my Facebook author page. To be informed of new releases and special offers, sign up for my newsletter or follow me on BookBub. And if you are interested in joining Dale Mayer's Reader Group, here is the Facebook sign up page.
http://geni.us/DaleMayerFBGroup

Cheers,
Dale Mayer

About the Author

Dale Mayer is a *USA Today* best-selling author, best known for her SEALs military romances, her Psychic Visions series, and her Lovely Lethal Garden cozy series. Her contemporary romances are raw and full of passion and emotion (Broken But … Mending, Hathaway House series). Her thrillers will keep you guessing (Kate Morgan, By Death series), and her romantic comedies will keep you giggling (*It's a Dog's Life*, a stand-alone novella; and the Broken Protocols series, starring Charming Marvin, the cat).

Dale honors the stories that come to her—and some of them are crazy, break all the rules and cross multiple genres!

To go with her fiction, she also writes nonfiction in many different fields, with books available on résumé writing, companion gardening, and the US mortgage system. All her books are available in print and ebook format.

Connect with Dale Mayer Online

Dale's Website – www.dalemayer.com
Twitter – @DaleMayer
Facebook Page – geni.us/DaleMayerFBFanPage
Facebook Group – geni.us/DaleMayerFBGroup
BookBub – geni.us/DaleMayerBookbub
Instagram – geni.us/DaleMayerInstagram
Goodreads – geni.us/DaleMayerGoodreads
Newsletter – geni.us/DaleNews

www.ingramcontent.com/pod-product-compliance
Lightning Source LLC
Chambersburg PA
CBHW070343200726

48294CB00003B/767